KINGFISHER•TREASURIES

Ideal for reading aloud with younger children, or for more experienced readers to enjoy independently, Kingfisher *Treasuries* offer the very best writing for children. Carefully chosen by expert compilers, the selection in each book is varied and wide-ranging. There are modern stories, traditional folk tales and fables, stories from a variety of cultures around the world, as well as work from exciting contemporary authors.

Popular with both children and their parents, the books in the *Treasury* series provide a useful introduction to new authors and encourage children to take pleasure in reading.

KINGFISHER
Larousse Kingfisher Chambers Inc.
95 Madison Avenue
New York, New York 10016

First edition 1995
2 4 6 8 10 9 7 5 3

LIBRARY OF CONGRESS CATALOGING-IN-PUBLICATION DATA
A treasury of stories for eight year olds / compiled by Edward Blishen
illustrated by Mick Reid.
—1st American ed.
p.   cm.
Summary: A collection of traditional and modern stories from around the
world by such authors as Edward Blishen, Astrid Lindgren.
1. Children's stories. [1. Short stories.]
I. Blishen, Edward, II. Reid, Mick, ill.
PZ5. T7555 1995
[Fic]—dc20 94-30241
CIP AC

ISBN 1-85697-545-2
Printed and bound in Great Britain by
BPC Consumer Books Ltd
A member of
The British Printing Company Ltd

Acknowledgments

For permission to reproduce copyright material acknowledgment and thanks are due to the following:

James Berry: Henry Holt & Co. Inc. for "Mrs. Dog First-Child and Monkey-Mother" from *Anancy Spiderman*
by James Berry. Text copyright © 1988 by James Berry. Illustrations copyright © 1988 by Joseph Olubo.
Published in the U.K. by Walker Books Ltd. and in the U.S.A. by Henry Holt & Co. Inc.; text copyright ©
James Berry 1988, illustrations copyright © Joseph Olubo 1988. Ruskin Bond: Macmillan Children's Books
for "The Day Grandfather Tickled a Tiger" from *Allsorts Five* by Ruskin Bond, Macmillan 1972. Copyright ©
Ruskin Bond 1972. Ted Hughes: Faber & Faber Ltd. for "How the Bee Became" from *How the Whale Became
and Other Stories* by Ted Hughes, Faber & Faber Ltd. 1963. Copyright © Ted Hughes 1963. Dick King-Smith:
A. P. Watt Ltd. on behalf of Fox Busters Ltd. for "A Narrow Squeak" from *A Narrow Squeak and Other Animal
Stories* by Dick King-Smith, Viking 1993. Copyright © Fox Busters Ltd. 1933. Laurie Lee: Peters Fraser &
Dunlop Group Ltd. for "My Birthday" by Laurie Lee. Copyright © Laurie Lee 1969. Astrid Lindgren: Astrid
Lindgren for "When Emil Got His Head Stuck in the Soup Tureen" from *Emil and the Soup Tureen* by Astrid
Lindgren, Hodder and Stoughton. Copyright © Astrid Lindgren 1963. Penelope Lively: Penguin Books
U.S.A. Inc. for "Uninvited Ghosts" from *Uninvited Ghosts and Other Stories* by Penelope Lively, William
Heinemann Ltd. Copyright © Penelope Lively. Alison Lurie: Reed Consumer Books Ltd. and HarperCollins
Inc. for "Kate Crackernuts" from *Clever Gretchen and Other Stories* by Alison Lurie, William Heinemann Ltd.
1980. Copyright © Alison Lurie 1980. Morris Lurie: Morris Lurie for "The Talking Bow-Tie" by Morris
Lurie from *Family Treasures and Other Bedtime Stories*, Hamish Hamilton 1990. Copyright © Morris Lurie.
Margaret Mahy: J. M. Dent & Sons Ltd. for "The House of Colored Windows" from *The Door in the Air and
Other Stories* by Margaret Mahy, first published by J. M. Dent & Sons Ltd. 1988. Copyright © Margaret Mahy
1988. Robert Newton Peck: Alfred A. Knopf Inc. for "A Barrel of Chicken" from *Soup* by Robert Newton
Peck. Copyright © Robert Newton Peck 1974. Roger Squire: Penguin Books Ltd. for "Moving Day" retold
by Roger Squire from *Wizards and Wampum—Legends of the Iroquois*, Blackie & Sons Ltd. Copyright ©
Roger Squire. Scholastic Publications Ltd. for "The King and the 'K'" by Emily Smith from *The Story of the
Year 1993*. Copyright © Emily Smith.

Every effort has been made to obtain permission from copyright holders. If any omissions have been made, we
shall be pleased to make suitable corrections in any reprint.

A TREASURY
OF STORIES
FOR
EIGHT
YEAR OLDS

Chosen by
EDWARD AND NANCY BLISHEN

Illustrated by
MICK REID

Kingfisher
NEW YORK

CONTENTS

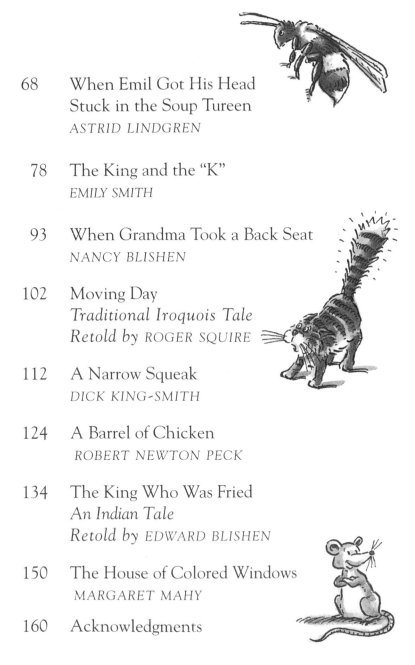

MY BIRTHDAY

Laurie Lee

I know I was eight because it was my birthday and I was allowed to play on the piano. My mother was showing me how to stretch an octave; eight smooth white notes like the teeth of a sheep: "One each for each year of your life."

"Let him play on the black ones," said my eldest sister. "One each for the color of his neck."

I couldn't stretch all the eight notes anyway, my fingers were still too short. But I could hit a dozen at once by bashing with my fist and the noise was splendid and awful.

"Our mother, does he have to . . . ?" My sisters huddled in a corner, but there wasn't much they could do. Today was my birthday and I was king, and nobody was allowed to be cross. So they searched through their boxes and found me three

7

pennies and told me to go out and buy myself something.

I'd been wanting to go anyway, because this meant walking to the shop and I wanted to show myself off. Something important had happened to me. I could feel it all over my body, and I wanted the world to know it. Yesterday I was seven—an infant, a nothing; today I was an eight-year-old man. There was a huge heap of difference between seven and eight. You could tell it just by saying the words. "Seven" was soppy, snoozy, and whimpering; "Eight" was solid, stout, and upright, sturdy as a granite gatepost. When you were seven elder sisters took liberties with you, when you were eight they had to be careful.

So this morning I walked through the village with dignity, neither whistling nor scuffling my boots.

Being eight, I decided, called for a new kind of behavior, something the grown-ups would understand. No more scratching, thought I—so I pulled my cap over my ears; no more sniffing—I blew my nose in a dock leaf. I felt larger and wiser than I had done yesterday and full of solemn thoughts. The villagers, of course, as soon as they saw me, would recognize the change. The old men would take off their hats and bow, the women murmur a respectful "Good morning;" perhaps the vicar would stop and invite me to tea, or the farmer ask my opinion of the weather.

In fact the first man I met was Grinder Davies, who'd been out cutting grass in the graveyard. "Hello, shorty," he said. "Take care how you go. There's a lot land out of doors this morning." I looked all around me and it was true enough. But when you were eight you didn't have to be told.

The three pennies in my hand were now wet as pebbles and as hot as little pancakes. I couldn't put them in my pocket because it was full of corn for my pigeons, so I spread them on the wall to dry. As this was bound to take time I climbed up beside them and stood for a while on my head. Upside down I saw the vicar walk right past my nose, but I don't think he recognized me.

Passing Spud Green's, the farmer, I stopped to chew on his railings, which tasted of resin and snails. The school railings, up the road, tasted of milk and boot polish, and the signpost of flashlight batteries. Each one, though different, never changed its flavor. I didn't know which I liked best. Farmer Green came out while I was tasting his railings but he didn't mention the weather. In fact he didn't say anything, he just hit the post with his stick, which rattled every tooth in my head.

It seemed miles to the store, having to walk slow and grown-up. In the end I got a bit bored. So I pulled my woolen jersey up over my head and pretended I was walking at night. The little sparks of sunshine that came through the wool looked like a sky of winter stars, and by wriggling and peering down an empty sleeve I could even make a crumpled moon . . .

I went Bump. There was a scream; and I could smell the store—lemon essence and candles and custard. Miss Jugg, who kept it, was pretending to be frightened. "I thought you were a bogey-man!"

I gave her my pennies and asked for a dozen Spearmintoes, each one guaranteed to last an hour.

"Spearmintoes on a Tuesday? Wherever did you get the money?"

"It's my birthday," I said. "I'm eight."

"He's eight," said Miss Jugg. "Well, the little lamb." And she gave me eight jelly beans, free.

I buried them in a cocoa tin on my way back home; and they're still there for all I know.

UNINVITED GHOSTS

Penelope Lively

Marian and Simon were sent to bed early on the day that the Brown family moved house. By then everyone had lost their temper with everyone else; the cat had been sick on the sitting room carpet; the dog had run away twice. If you have ever moved you will know what kind of a day it had been. Packing cases and newspaper all over the place . . . sandwiches instead of proper meals . . . the kettle lost and a closet stuck on the stairs and Mrs. Brown's favorite vase broken. There was bread and baked beans for supper, the television wouldn't work and the water wasn't hot so when all was said and done the children didn't object too violently to being packed off to bed. They'd had enough, too. They had one last argument about who was going to sleep by the window, put on their pajamas, got into bed, switched the lights out . . . and it was at that point that the ghost came out of the bottom drawer of the chest of drawers.

It oozed out, a gray cloudy shape about three feet long smelling faintly of woodsmoke, sat down on a chair and began to hum to itself. It looked like a bundle of bedclothes, except that it was not solid: you could see, quite clearly, the cushion on the chair beneath it.

Marian gave a shriek. "That's a ghost!"

"Oh, be quiet, dear, do," said the ghost. "That noise goes right through my head. And it's not nice to call people names." It took out a ball of yarn and some needles and began to knit.

What would you have done? Well, yes—Simon and Marian did just that and I daresay you can imagine what happened. You try telling your mother that you can't get to sleep because there's a ghost sitting in the room clacking its knitting needles and humming. Mrs. Brown said the kind of things she could be expected to say and the ghost continued sitting there knitting and humming and Mrs. Brown went out, banging the door and saying threatening things about if there's so much as another word from either of you . . .

"She can't see it," said Marian to Simon.

"'Course not, dear," said the ghost. "It's the kiddies I'm here for. Love kiddies, I do. We're going to be ever such friends."

"Go away!" yelled Simon. "This is our house now!"

"No, it isn't," said the ghost smugly. "Always been here, I have. A hundred years and more. Seen plenty of families come and go, I have. Go to bye-byes now, there's good children."

The children glared at it and buried themselves under the bedclothes. And, eventually, slept.

The next night it was there again. This time it was smoking a long white pipe and reading a newspaper dated 1842. Beside it was a second gray cloudy shape. "Hello, dearies," said the ghost. "Say how do you do to my Auntie Edna."

"She can't come here too," wailed Marian.

"Oh yes she can," said the ghost. "Always comes here in August, does Auntie. She likes a change."

Auntie Edna was even worse, if possible. She sucked peppermint drops that smelled so strong that Mrs. Brown, when she came to kiss the children good night, looked suspiciously under their pillows. She also sang hymns in a loud squeaky voice. The children lay there groaning and the ghosts sang and rustled the newspapers and ate peppermints.

The next night there were three of them. "Meet Uncle Charlie!" said the first ghost. The children groaned.

"And Jip," said the ghost. "Here, Jip, good dog—come and say hello to the kiddies, then." A large gray dog that you could see straight through came out from under the bed, wagging its tail. The cat, who had been curled up beside Marian's feet (it was supposed to sleep in the kitchen, but there are always ways for a resourceful cat to get what it wants), gave a howl and shot on top of the wardrobe, where it sat spitting. The dog lay down in the middle of the rug and set about scratching

itself vigorously; evidently it had ghost fleas, too.

Uncle Charlie was unbearable. He had a loud cough that kept going off like a machine gun and he told the longest most pointless stories the children had ever heard. He said he too loved kiddies and he knew kiddies loved stories. In the middle of the seventh story the children went to sleep out of sheer boredom.

The following week the ghosts left the bedroom and were to be found all over the house. The children had no peace at all. They'd be quietly doing their homework and all of a sudden Auntie Edna would be breathing down their necks reciting arithmetic tables. The original ghost took to sitting on top of the television with his legs in front of the picture. Uncle Charlie told his stories all through the best programs and the dog

lay permanently at the top of the stairs. The Browns' cat became quite hysterical, refused to eat, and went to live on the top shelf of the kitchen dresser.

Something had to be done. Marian and Simon also were beginning to show the effects; their mother decided they looked peaky and bought an appalling sticky brown vitamin medicine from the drugstore to strengthen them. "It's the ghosts!" wailed the children. "We don't need vitamins!" Their mother said severely that she didn't want to hear another word of this silly nonsense about ghosts. Auntie Edna, who was sitting smirking on the other side of the kitchen table at that very moment, nodded vigorously and took out a packet of mints which she sucked noisily.

"We've got to get them to go and live somewhere else," said Marian. But where, that was the problem, and how? It was then that they had a bright idea. On Sunday the Browns were all going to see their uncle who was rather rich and lived alone in a big house with thick carpets everywhere and empty rooms and the biggest color television you ever saw. Plenty of room for ghosts.

They were very cunning. They suggested to the ghosts that they might like a drive in the country. The ghosts said at first that they were quite comfortable where they were, thank you, and they didn't fancy these newfangled motor-cars, not at their time of life. But then Auntie Edna remembered that she liked looking at the pretty flowers and the trees and finally they agreed to give it a try. They sat in a row on the back shelf of the car. Mrs. Brown kept asking why there was such a

strong smell of peppermint and Mr. Brown kept roaring at Simon and Marian to keep still while he was driving. The fact was that the ghosts were shoving them; it was like being nudged by three cold damp washcloths. And the ghost dog, who had come along too of course, was carsick.

When they got to Uncle Dick's the ghosts came in and had a look round. They liked the expensive carpets and the enormous television. They slid in and out of the closets and walked through the doors and the walls and sent Uncle Dick's parakeets into a decline from which they have never recovered. Nice place, they said, nice and comfy.

"Why not stay here?" said Simon, in an offhand tone.

"Couldn't do that," said the ghosts firmly. "No kiddies. Dull. We like a place with a bit of life to it." And they piled back into the car and sang hymns all the way home to the Browns' house. They also ate toast. There were real toast crumbs on the floor and the children got the blame.

Simon and Marian were in despair. The ruder they were to the ghosts the more the ghosts liked it. "Cheeky!" they said indulgently. "What a cheeky little pair of kiddies! There now . . . come

19

and give Uncle a kiss." The children weren't even safe in the bath. One or other of the ghosts would come and sit on the taps and talk to them. Uncle Charlie had produced a mouth organ and played the same tune over and over again; it was quite excruciating. The children went around with their hands over their ears. Mrs. Brown took them to the doctor to find out if there was something wrong with their hearing. The children knew better than to say anything to the doctor about the ghosts. It was pointless saying anything to anyone.

I don't know what would have happened if Mrs. Brown hadn't happened to make friends with Mrs. Walker from down the road. Mrs. Walker had twin babies, and one day she brought the babies along for tea.

Now one baby is bad enough. Two babies are trouble in a big way. These babies created pandemonium. When they weren't both howling they were crawling around the floor pulling the tablecloths off the tables or hitting their heads on the chairs and hauling the books out of the book-cases. They threw their food all over the kitchen and flung cups of milk on the floor. Their mother mopped up after them and every time she tried to have a conversation with Mrs. Brown the babies bawled in chorus so that no one could hear a word.

In the middle of this the ghosts appeared. One

baby was yelling its head off and the other was gluing pieces of chewed up bread onto the front of the television. The ghosts swooped down on them with happy cries. "Oh!" they trilled. "Bless their little hearts then, diddums, give Auntie a smile then." And the babies stopped in mid-howl and gazed at the ghosts. The ghosts cooed at the babies and the babies cooed at the ghosts. The ghosts chattered to the babies and sang them songs and the babies chattered back and were as good as gold for the next hour and their mother had the first proper conversation she'd had in weeks. When they went the ghosts stood in a row at the window, waving.

Simon and Marian knew when to seize an opportunity. That evening they had a talk with the ghosts. At first the ghosts raised objections.

They didn't fancy the idea of moving, they said; you got set in your ways, at their age; Auntie Edna reckoned a strange house would be the death of her.

The children talked about the babies, relentlessly.

And the next day they led the ghosts down the road, followed by the ghost dog, and into the Walkers' house. Mrs. Walker doesn't know to this day why the babies, who had been screaming for the last half hour, suddenly stopped and broke into great smiles. And she has never understood why, from that day forth, the babies became the most tranquil, quiet, amiable babies in the area. The ghosts kept the babies amused from morning to night. The babies thrived; the ghosts were happy; the ghost dog, who was actually a female, settled down so well that she had puppies which is one of the most surprising aspects of the whole business. The Brown children heaved a sigh of relief and got back to normal life. The babies, though, I have to tell you, grew up somewhat peculiar.

HOW THE BEE BECAME

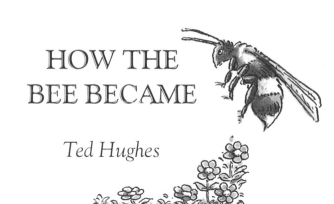

Ted Hughes

Now in the middle of the Earth lived a demon. This demon spent all his time groping about in the dark tunnels, searching for precious metals and gems.

He was hunchbacked and knobbly-armed. His ears draped over his shoulders like a wrinkly cloak. These kept him safe from the bits of rock that were always falling from the ceilings of his caves. He had only one eye, which was a fire. To keep this fire alive he had to feed it with gold and silver. Over this eye he cooked his dinner every night. It is hard to say what he ate. All kinds of fungus that grew in the airless dark on the rocks. His

drink was mostly tar and oil, which he loved. There is no end of tar and oil in the middle of the Earth.

He rarely came up to the light. Once, when he did, he saw the creatures that God was making.

"What's this?" he cried, when a grasshopper landed on his clawed, horny foot. Then he saw Lion. Then Cobra. Then, far above him, Eagle.

"My word!" he said, and hurried back down into his dark caves to think about what he had seen.

He was jealous of the beautiful things that God was making.

"I will make something," he said at last, "which will be far more beautiful than any of God's creatures."

But he had no idea how to set about it.

So one day he crept up to God's workshop and watched God at work. He peeped from behind the door. He saw him model the clay, bake it in the sun's fire, then breathe life into it. So that was it!

Away he dived, back down into the center of the Earth.

At the center of the Earth it was too hot for clay. Everything was already baked hard. He set about trying to make his own clay.

First, he ground up rocks between his palms. That was powder. But how was he to make it into clay? He needed water, and there in the center of the Earth it was too hot for water.

He searched and he searched, but there was none. At last he sat down. He felt so sad he began to cry. Big tears rolled down his nose.

"If only I had water," he sobbed, "this clay could become a real living creature. Why do I have to live where there is no water?"

He looked at the powder in his palm, and began to cry afresh. As he looked and wept, and looked and wept, a tear fell off the end of his nose straight into the powder.

But he was too late. A demon's tears are no ordinary tears. There was a red flash, a fizz, a bubbling, and where the powder had been was nothing but a dark stain on his palm.

He felt like weeping again. Now he had water, but no powder.

"So much for stone powder," he said. "I need something stronger."

Then quickly, before his tears dried, he ground some of the precious metal that he used to feed the fire of his eye. As soon as it was powder he wetted it with a tear off his cheek. But it was no better than the stone powder had been. There was a flash, a fizz, a bubbling, and nothing.

"Well," he said. "What now?"

At last he thought of it—he would make a powder of precious gems. It was hard work grinding these, but at last he had finished. Now for a tear. But he was too excited to cry. He struggled to bring up a single tear. It was no good. His eye was dry as an oven. He struggled and he struggled. Nothing! All at once he sat down and burst into tears.

"It's no good!" he cried. "I can't cry!" Then he felt his tears wet on his cheeks.

"I'm crying!" he cried joyfully. "Quick, quick!" And he splashed a tear on to the powder of the precious gems. The result was perfect. He had made a tiny piece of beautiful clay. Only tiny, because his tears had been few. But it was big enough.

"Now," he said, "what kind of creature shall I make?"

The jewel clay was very hard to work into shape. It was tough as red-hot iron.

So he laid the clay on his anvil and began to beat it into shape with his great hammer.

He beat and beat and beat that clay for a thousand years.

And at last it was shaped. Now it needed baking. Very carefully, because the thing he had made was very frail, he put it into the fire of his eye to bake.

Then, beside a great heap of small pieces of gold and silver, for another thousand years he sat, feeding the fire of his eye with the precious metal. All this time, in the depths of his eye glowed his little creature, baking slowly.

At last it was baked.

Now came the real problem. How was he going to breathe life into it?

He puffed and he blew, but it was no good.

"It is so beautiful!" he cried. "I must give it life!"

It certainly was beautiful. All the precious gems

of which it was made mingled their colors. And from the flames in which it had been baked, it had taken a dark fire. It gleamed and flashed: red, blue, orange, green, purple, no bigger than your fingernail.

But it had no life.

There was only one thing to do. He must go to God and ask him to breathe life into it.

When God saw the demon he was amazed. He had no idea that such a creature existed.

"Who are you?" he asked. "Where have you come from?"

The demon hung his head. "Now," he thought, "I will use a trick."

"I'm a jewelsmith," he said humbly. "And I live in the center of the Earth. I have brought you a present, to show my respect for you."

He showed God the little creature that he had made. God was amazed again.

"How beautiful!" he kept saying as he turned it over and over on his hand. "How beautiful! What a wonderfully clever smith you are."

"Ah!" said the demon. "But not so clever as you. I could never breathe life into it. If you had made it, it would be alive. As it is, it is beautiful, but dead."

God was flattered. "That's soon altered," he said. He raised the demon's gift to his lips and breathed life into it.

Then he held it out. It crawled onto the end of his finger.

"Buzz!" it went, and whirred its thin, beautiful wings. Like a flash, the demon snatched it from God's fingertip and plunged back down into the center of the earth.

There, for another thousand years, he lay, letting the little creature crawl over his fingers and make short flights from one hand to the other. It glittered all its colors in the light of his eye's fire. The demon was very happy.

"You are more beautiful than any of God's creatures," he crooned.

But life was hard for the little creature down in the center of the Earth, with no one to play with but the demon. He had God's breath in him, and he longed to be among the other creatures under the sun.

And he was sad for another reason. In his veins ran not blood, but the tears with which the demon had mixed his clay. And what is sadder than a tear? Feeling the sadness in all his veins, he moved restlessly over the demon's hands.

One day the demon went up to the light to compare his little creature with the ones God had made.

"Buzz!" went his pet, and was away over a mountain.

"Come back!" roared the demon, then quickly covered his mouth with his hands, frightened that God would hear him. He began to search for his creature, but soon, frightened that God would see him, he crept back into the Earth.

Still his little creature was not happy.

The sadness of the demon's tears was always in him. It was part of him. It was what flowed in his veins.

"If I gather everything that is sweet and bright and happy," he said to himself, "that should make me feel better. Here there are plenty of wonderful sweet, bright, happy things."

And he began to fly from flower to flower, collecting the bright, sunny sweetness out of their cups.

"Ah!" he cried. "Wonderful!"

The sweetness lit up his body. He felt the sun glowing through him from what he drank. For the first time in his life he felt happy.

But the moment he stopped drinking from the flowers, the sadness came creeping back along his veins and the gloom into his thoughts.

"That demon made me of tears," he said. "How can I ever hope to get away from the sadness of tears? Unless I never leave these flowers."

And he hurried from flower to flower.

He could never stop, and it was too good to stop.

Soon, he had drunk so much, the sweetness began to ooze out of his pores. He was so full of it, he was brimming over with it. And every second he drank more.

At last he had to pause.

"I must store all this somewhere," he said.

So he made a hive, and all the sweetness that oozed from him he stored in that hive. Man found it and called it honey. God saw what the little creature was doing, and blessed him, and called him Bee.

But Bee must still go from flower to flower, seeking sweetness. The tears of the demon are still in his veins ready to make him gloomy the moment he stops drinking from the flowers. When he is angry and stings, the smart of his sting is the tear of the demon. If he has to keep that sweet, it is no wonder that he drinks sweetness until he brims over.

THE TALKING BOW TIE

Morris Lurie

That evening, Mr. Baxter brought home a brand-new bow tie.

"Oh, very lovely!" said Mrs. Baxter, and it was.

It was the boldest bright yellow with the biggest purple spots, and it looked very happy and gay.

"I thought I'd wear it tonight," said Mr. Baxter.

Mr. and Mrs. Baxter were going out to dinner.

So, Mr. Baxter had a shower, and then he put on a nice clean white shirt (and his underwear and pants and shoes and socks, too, of course), and then he popped himself in front of the big mirror in the bathroom and put on the brand-new bow tie.

"Oh, yes indeed!" he said, giving it a little straighten this way and that. "Very elegant!"

"Very elegant?" said the bow tie.

"What?" said Mr. Baxter.

"You don't look very elegant," said the bow tie. "You look ridiculous."

"I beg your pardon?" said Mr. Baxter.

"You are one of the most ridiculous-looking people I have ever seen," said the bow tie.

"Mary!" cried Mr. Baxter, running out of the bathroom. "Mary! This bow tie just spoke to me! It said I looked ridiculous!"

Mrs. Baxter was busy in the kitchen preparing dinner for the children, and she didn't really hear what Mr. Baxter said.

"Well, wear something else, dear," she said, serving up the children's lamb chops.

"What?" said Mr. Baxter. "Oh. All right."

And he took off the bow tie and put on his favorite pale blue tie instead, which was very nice and had no spots at all.

The next morning, when she was doing the cleaning, Mrs. Baxter saw the brand-new bow tie lying on the dressing table, where Mr. Baxter had dropped it.

"Oh, how pretty!" she said, not remembering a single thing about it. She picked it up and held it to her hair. "I think it suits me," she said. "Yes, I think I'll wear it this afternoon when I go shopping."

"Your nose is too long," said the bow tie.

"I beg your pardon?" said Mrs. Baxter.

"It looks like a sausage," said the bow tie. "And your eyes are too small, too. They look like shriveled raisins."

"What?" said Mrs. Baxter.

"In fact," said the bow tie, "your face is one of the silliest faces I have ever seen."

"Oh, you horrid thing!" cried Mrs. Baxter, and she flung the bow tie as far away as she could, out into the hall.

Now, the Baxters had two children, a boy and a girl. The boy's name was Michael. And at four o'clock that afternoon he came home, as usual, from school.

"Hi!" he called. "Anyone home?"

There was a note on the kitchen table.

Gone to have my hair done, it said. *Be back soon.*
There are some lovely new apples in the fruit bowl.
  Love, Mother.

So, Michael took an apple and started to munch it, and then he saw the brand-new bow tie lying on the floor in the hall.

"Hey, what a great bow tie!" he said, picking it up. "I think I'll wear it to school tomorrow!"

"Don't be ridiculous," said the bow tie.

"What?" said Michael. "Who said that?"

"Your head's like a garbage can with the lid jammed on crooked," said the bow tie.

"Get out of it!" said Michael.

"And the rest of you doesn't look too hot, either, if you want to know the truth," said the bow tie.

"I don't need this!" cried Michael, and he threw the bow tie down and went for a long, long ride on his bike.

Then Michael's sister came home. Her name was Suzie. She picked the bow tie up at once.

"Oh, how gorgeous!" she said.

"But you're not," said the bow tie.

"Did you say something?" said Suzie.

"You've got a face like a pickled pillow," said the bow tie. "And your ears look like jug handles poking out of your head."

"Well, I don't like you either," said Suzie, and she threw the bow tie over her shoulder and went off to her room to read a good book.

Now, the Baxters had a dog, a very floppy and friendly dog, and his name was Ebenezer.

"I know," said Mrs. Baxter when she came home. "I'll give that bow tie to Ebenezer. It wouldn't dare say anything to him."

And she tied the bow tie very carefully around Ebenezer's neck.

"Yes," she said. "Quite nice."

"What a smelly dog," said the bow tie. "He smells like an over-cooked cabbage. He smells like a pair of old socks."

"Woof!" cried Ebenezer, and he tore off the bow tie and ran under the sofa in the front room and wouldn't come out all night.

The last member of the Baxter family to try the bow tie was the family cat. She was small and white and fluffy and her name was Daphne, and I don't know how she came to wear the bow tie, but she did.

"What a silly looking cat," said the bow tie. "You look like a moldy cheese. You look like a cross-eyed mop."

"Meow!" cried Daphne, and she snatched off the bow tie and flew straight up the tallest tree in the garden and absolutely refused to come down, even for her supper.

"This has gone on quite long enough!" said Mr. Baxter. "That bow tie is totally terrible! It has insulted everyone! It must be taught a lesson at once! There is only one thing to do!"

And he put it in the refrigerator, in the freezer part, next to the fish sticks, and he left it there for three whole days and nights.

And when he took it out, believe you me, that talking bow tie never spoke again.

THE ONE THAT GOT AWAY

Jan Mark

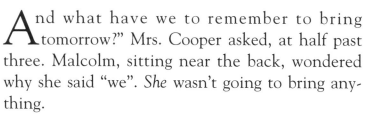

A nd what have we to remember to bring tomorrow?" Mrs. Cooper asked, at half past three. Malcolm, sitting near the back, wondered why she said "we". *She* wasn't going to bring anything.

"Something interesting, Mrs. Cooper," said everyone else, all together.

"And what are we going to do then?"

"Stand up and talk about it, Mrs. Cooper."

"So don't forget. All right. Chairs on tables. Good-bye, Class Four."

"Good-bye, Mrs. Cooper. Good-bye, everybody."

It all came out ever so slow, like saying prayers in assembly. "Amen," said Malcolm, very quietly. Class Four put its chairs on the tables, collected its coats and went home, talking about all the interesting things it would bring into school tomorrow.

Malcolm walked by himself. Mrs. Cooper had first told them to find something interesting on Monday. Now it was Thursday and still he had not come up with any bright ideas. There were plenty of things that he found interesting, but the trouble was, they never seemed to interest anyone else. Last time this had happened he had brought along his favorite pebble and shown it to the class.

"Very nice, Malcolm," Mrs. Cooper had said. "Now tell us what's interesting about it." He hadn't known what to say. Surely anyone looking at the pebble could see how interesting it was.

Mary was going to bring her gerbil. James, Sarah and William had loudly discussed rare shells and fossils, and the only spider in the world with five legs.

"It can't be a spider then," said David, who was eavesdropping.

"It had an accident," William said.

Isobel intended to bring her pocket calculator and show them how it could write her name by punching in 738051 and turning it upside down. She did this every time, but it still looked interesting.

Malcolm could think of nothing.

When he reached home he went up to his bedroom and looked at the shelf where he kept important things: his twig that looked like a stick insect, his marble that looked like a glass eye, the penny with a hole in it and the Siamese twin jelly-beans,

one red, one green and stuck together, back to back. He noticed that they were now stuck to the shelf, too. His pebble had once been there as well, but after Class Four had said it was boring he had put it back in the garden. He still went to see it sometimes.

What he really needed was something that could move about, like Mary's gerbil or William's five-legged spider. He sat down on his bed and began to think.

On Friday, after assembly, Class Four began to be interesting. Mary kicked off with the gerbil that whirred round its cage like a hairy balloon with the air escaping. Then they saw William's lame spider, James's fossil, Jason's collection of snail shells stuck one on top of the other like the Leaning Tower of Pisa, and David's bottled conkers that he had kept in an airtight jar for three years. They were still as glossy as new shoes.

Then it was Malcolm's turn. He went up to the front and held out a matchbox. He had chosen it very carefully. It was the kind with the same label top and bottom so that when you opened it you could never be sure that it was the right way up and all the matches fell out. Malcolm opened it upside down and jumped. Mrs. Cooper jumped too. Malcolm threw himself down on hands and knees and looked under her desk.

"What's the matter?" Mrs. Cooper said.

"It's fallen out!" Malcolm cried.

"What is it?" Mrs. Cooper said, edging away.

"I don't know—it's got six legs and sharp knees . . . and sort of frilly eyebrows on stalks—" He pounced. "There it goes."

"Where?"

"Missed it," said Malcolm. "It's running under your chair, Mary."

"Mary squeaked and climbed on to the table because she thought that was the right way to behave when creepy-crawlies were about.

"I see it!" Jason yelled, and jumped up and down. David threw a book in the direction that Jason was pointing and James began beating the floor with a rolled up comic book.

"I got it—I killed it," he shouted.

"It's crawling up the curtains," Sarah said and Mrs. Cooper, who was standing by the curtains, moved rapidly away from them.

"It's over by the door," Mary shrieked, and several people ran to head it off. Chairs were over-turned.

Malcolm stood by Mrs. Cooper's desk with his matchbox. His contribution was definitely the most interesting thing that anyone had seen that morning. He was only sorry that he hadn't seen it himself.

KATE CRACKERNUTS

Alison Lurie

Once upon a time there was a king and a queen, such as there have been in many lands. The king had a daughter, and the queen had one also. And though they were no kin, yet the two girls loved each other better than sisters. But the queen was jealous because the king's daughter Ann was prettier than her own daughter Kate. She wished to find some way to spoil Ann's beauty; so she went to consult the henwife, who was a witch.

"Aye, I can help you," said the henwife. "Send her to me in the morning; but make sure she does not eat anything before she comes." And she put her big black pot on the fire, and boiled a sheep's hide and bones in it, with other nasty things.

Early in the morning the queen told Ann to go to the henwife and fetch some eggs. But as she left

the house, Ann took up a crust of bread to eat on the way. When she asked for the eggs, the witch said to her, "Lift the lid off that pot, and you will find what you need." So the king's daughter lifted the lid; but nothing came out of the pot except an evil smell. "Go back to your mother, and tell her to keep her pantry door better locked," said the henwife.

When the queen heard this message, she knew that Ann must have had something to eat. So she locked her pantry, and next morning sent the girl off again. But as Ann went through the garden she saw the gardener picking vegetables. Being a friendly girl, she stopped to speak with him, and he gave her a handful of peas to eat. And when she got to the henwife's house, everything happened just as before.

On the third morning the queen went down to the gate with Ann, so as to be certain she would eat noth- ing on her way to the witch. And this time, when Ann lifted the lid of the pot, off jumped her own pretty head, and on jumped a sheep's head in its place.

44

When the queen looked out her window and saw Ann coming back with her sheep's head, she laughed out loud with satisfaction. "Look at your sister," she said to her own daughter Kate. "Now you are the prettiest by far."

"That pleases me not," said Kate. And she would say no more to her mother, but wrapped a fine linen cloth around her sister's head, and took her by the hand, and they went out into the world together to seek their fortunes.

They walked on far, and farther than I can tell, eating the berries that grew by the roadside, and the nuts that Kate gathered in her apron and cracked as they went along. At last they came to a tall castle. Kate knocked at the castle door, and begged a night's lodging for herself and her sister.

Now the king and queen of that place had two sons, and the elder of them was ill with a strange wasting illness. Though he ate heartily, and slept late, yet every morning he was more thin and pale than the evening before. The king had offered a peck of gold to anyone who would sit up with his son for three nights and find out what ailed him. Many had tried, but all had failed. But Kate was a clever girl and a brave girl, and she offered to sit up with the prince. She did not go boldly into his room as the others had, but arranged to have herself hidden there in the evening, and watched to see what would happen.

Till midnight all was quiet. As twelve o'clock struck, however, the sick prince rose, dressed himself, and went downstairs. He walked as if in a dream, and did not seem to notice Kate following after him. He went to the stables, saddled his horse, called his hound, and mounted. Kate leaped up behind him, but he paid her no heed. Away went the horse with the prince and Kate through the greenwood, where the nuts were ripe. As they passed under the trees, Kate picked the nuts and filled her apron with them, for she did not know when they might come back again.

They rode on and on, till they came to a green hill. There the prince drew rein and spoke for the first time, saying, "Open, open, green hill, and let in the young prince with his horse and his hound."

And Kate added, "and his lady behind him."

Then the hill opened, and they passed into a great hall filled with bright light that seemed to come from nowhere, and a strange music playing. Kate slipped down off the horse, and hid herself behind the door.

At once the prince was surrounded by fairy ladies who led him off to the dance. All night he danced without stopping, first with one and then with another, and though he looked weary and worn they would not let him leave off.

At last the cock crew, and the prince made haste to mount his horse. Kate jumped up behind,

and they rode home, where the prince lay down to sleep paler and more ill than before.

The next night when the clock struck twelve the same thing happened; and again Kate rode through the forest behind the prince into the green hill. This time she did not watch the dancing, but crept near to where some of the fairy people were sitting together and a fairy baby was playing with a wand.

"What news in the world above?" said one.

"No news," said the other, "but that a sad lady with a sheep's head has come to lodge in the castle."

"Is that so?" said the first, laughing. "If only she knew that three strokes of that wand would make her as fair as she ever was."

Kate heard this, and thought that she must have the wand. She took some nuts and rolled them toward the baby from behind the door, till the baby ran after the nuts and let the wand fall, and Kate snatched it up and put it in her apron. At cockcrow she rode home as before, and the prince lay down to sleep, looking weary and ill unto death. Kate ran to her room and tapped her sister Ann three times with the wand; and the sheep's head jumped off and Ann had her own pretty head again. Then Ann dressed herself and went into the great hall of the castle where all welcomed her, and the king's younger son thought that he had never seen anyone sweeter and prettier in his life.

On the third night, Kate watched the sick prince again, and rode behind him to the green hill. Again she hid behind the door and listened to the talk of the fairy people. This time the little child was playing with a yellow bird.

"What news in the world above?" said one fairy to the other.

"No news, but that the king and queen are at their wits' end to know what ails their eldest son."

"Is that so?" said the first fairy, laughing. "If only they knew that three bites of that birdie would free him from the spell and make him as well as ever he was."

Kate heard this, and thought that she must have the yellow birdie. So she rolled nuts to the baby until he ran after them and dropped the birdie, and she caught it up and put it in her apron.

At cockcrow they set off for home again, and as soon as they got there Kate plucked and cooked

the yellow birdie and took it to the prince. He was lying in bed more dead than alive after his night's dancing; but when he smelled the dish, he opened his eyes and said, "Oh, I wish I had a bite of that birdie!" So Kate gave him a bite, and he rose up on his elbow.

By and by he cried out again, "Oh, if only I had another bite of that birdie!" Kate gave him another bite, and the prince sat up on his bed and looked about him. Then he said again, "Oh, if only I had a third bite of that birdie!" Kate gave him a third bite, and he got out of bed, well and strong again. He dressed himself and sat down by the fire, and Kate told him all that had passed. They stayed there till it was full morning, and the people of the castle came in and found them cracking nuts together.

So Kate married the king's eldest son, and Ann married his brother, and they lived happily together ever after.

THE DAY GRANDFATHER TICKLED A TIGER

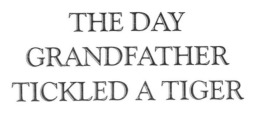

Ruskin Bond

Timothy, our tiger cub, was found by my grandfather on a hunting expedition in the Terai jungles near Dehra, in northern India. Because Grandfather lived in Dehra and so knew the jungles well, he was persuaded to accompany the hunting party, consisting of several government officials from Delhi, to advise on the terrain and the directions the beaters should take once a tiger had been spotted. A tiger, of course, was the hunters' chief target.

They never got their tiger, but Grandfather, strolling down a forest path some distance from the main party, discovered a little tiger about eighteen inches long, hidden among the roots of a banyan tree. After the expedition ended, Grandfather took the beast home to Dehra, where Grandmother gave him the name Timothy.

Timothy's favorite place in the house was the living room. He would snuggle down comfortably on the sofa, reclining there with serene dignity and snarling only when anyone tried to take his place. One of his chief amusements was to stalk whoever was playing with him, and so, when I went to live with my grandparents, I became one of the tiger's pets. With a crafty look in his eyes, and his body in a deep crouch, he would creep closer and closer to me, suddenly making a dash for my feet. Then, rolling on his back and kicking with delight, he would pretend to bite my ankles.

By this time he was the size of a full-grown golden retriever, and when I took him for walks in Dehra, people on the road would give us a wide berth. Nights he slept in the quarters of our cook, Mahmoud. "One of these days," Grandmother declared, "we are going to find Timothy sitting on Mahmoud's bed and no sign of Mahmoud!"

When Timothy was about six months old, his stalking became more serious and he had to be chained up more frequently. Even the household started to mistrust him and, when he began to trail Mahmoud around the house with what looked like villainous intent, Grandfather decided it was time to transfer the animal to a zoo.

The nearest zoo was at Lucknow, some 200 miles away. Grandfather reserved a first-class compartment for himself and Timothy and set forth. The Lucknow zoo authorities were only too pleased to receive a well-fed and fairly civilized tiger.

Grandfather had no opportunity to see how Timothy was getting on in his new home until about six months later when he and Grandmother visited relatives in Lucknow. Grandfather went to the zoo and directly to Timothy's cage. The tiger was there, crouched in a corner, full-grown, his magnificent striped coat gleaming with health.

"Hello, Timothy," Grandfather said.

Climbing the railing, he put his arm through the bars of the cage. Timothy approached, and allowed Grandfather to put both arms about his head. Grandfather stroked the tiger's forehead and tickled his ears. Each time Timothy growled, Grandfather gave him a smack across the mouth, which

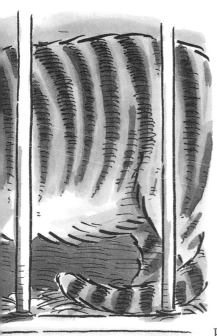

had been his way of keeping the animal quiet when he lived with us.

Timothy licked Grandfather's hands. The tiger showed nervousness, springing away when a leopard in the next cage snarled at him, but Grandfather shooed the leopard off and Timothy returned to licking his hands. Every now and then the leopard would rush at the bars, and Timothy would again slink back to a neutral corner.

A number of people had gathered to watch the reunion, when a keeper pushed his way through the crowd and asked Grandfather what he was doing. "I'm talking to Timothy," said Grandfather. "Weren't you here when I gave him to the zoo six months ago?"

"I haven't been here very long," said the surprised keeper. "Please continue your conversation. I have never been able to touch that tiger myself. I find him very bad-tempered."

Grandfather had been stroking and slapping Timothy for about five minutes when he noticed another keeper observing him with some alarm. Grandfather recognized him as the keeper who had been there when he had delivered Timothy to the zoo. "You remember me," said Grandfather. "Why don't you transfer Timothy to a different cage, away from this stupid leopard?"

"But—sir," stammered the keeper, "it is not your tiger."

"I realize that he is no longer mine," said Grandfather testily. "But at least take my suggestion."

"I remember your tiger very well," said the keeper. "He died two months ago."

"Died!" exclaimed Grandfather.

"Yes, sir, of pneumonia. This tiger was trapped in the hills only last month, and he is very dangerous!"

The tiger was still licking Grandfather's arm and apparently enjoying it more all the time.

Grandfather withdrew his hand from the cage in a motion that seemed to take an age. With his face near the tiger's he mumbled, "Good night, Timothy." Then, giving the keeper a scornful look, Grandfather walked briskly out of the zoo.

MRS. DOG
FIRST-CHILD
AND
MONKEY-MOTHER

James Berry

Mrs. Dog's first child is clever, you see. From when she is small-small she can stand on her head and catch things with her feet. Swing-Swing will catch a big unhusked coconut with her feet, her lovely little dog-child's feet. Lots and lots of difficult acts Swing-Swing-Janey can perform for herself alone, or for a crowd.

Then one day, just before sunset, Monkey-Mother happens to see Swing-Swing-Janey playing alone.

Passing by, going home with her tribe of many children, with one on her back, Monkey-Mother stops. She stands there with child on her back, watching Janey.

Swing-Swing carries on. Swing-Swing is in front of her house, there at roadside, practicing her sticks-catching.

Swing-Swing tosses up four sticks and catches them. She keeps on doing that. Monkey-Mother is thrilled. Monkey-Mother grins.

Monkey-Mother puts down her child and settles down watching, with all her lots of children around her watching too.

Then so excited to have a crowd watching her, Swing-Swing-Janey starts up something different.

Swing-Swing tosses her ball up, then falls quick-quick onto her hands, throws her bottom end up, catches the ball with her feet, bends her knees, flicks the ball up again, half spins back onto her feet and catches the ball with her hands.

Seeing Swing-Swing's movements so precise, so perfect, the family grin and clap. And grinning and clapping Monkey-Mother says:

"O so right and so spry,
So nippy and so flippy!"

And grinning and clapping her lots of children say:

"O so right and so spry,
So nippy and so flippy!"

Swing-Swing-Janey repeats her act. Then Swing-Swing does lots of other things she can do.

The sun sets, and nobody sees Janey. Swing-Swing has disappeared.

Night comes down. No Swing-Swing-Janey is anywhere. Mrs. Dog stands outside and calls and

calls; no answer. No Swing-Swing comes home.

Mrs. Dog practically goes off her head with worry.

Mrs. Dog walks quickly to every neighbor and asks about Swing-Swing. Nobody has seen her child. Mrs. Dog approaches everybody passing her house. Nobody has seen Swing-Swing-Janey. Nobody knows to where the child has disappeared.

Then just before bedtime, Mrs. Puss calls and says, "I hear you lost your child. I have to say I did see your child. Monkey-Mother carried away your child. They all joked and laughed together, walking on and on together, like a friendly family."

"But where does Monkey-Mother live?" Mrs. Dog wants to know.

Mrs. Puss has no idea. Nobody knows where Monkey-Mother lives. She roams about; it is

known. She lives miles and miles away; it is believed.

Mrs. Dog begins to go about looking for her child, promptly.

Many strange villages see Mrs. Dog for the first time.

Mrs. Dog sees tailors making clothes, shoemakers making shoes, tinsmiths making vessels. Each time Mrs. Dog asks the people, "Have you seen a dog-child with Monkey-Mother?"

"No," they say.

"Do you know where Monkey-Mother lives?"

"No," they say.

Every person or group of people Mrs. Dog meets she asks the same questions and gets the same answers.

Mrs. Dog keeps on going with her traveling and her looking. Other strange villages see Mrs. Dog for the first time.

She sees basketmakers making baskets, carvers

carving wood, potters making pots. Each time Mrs. Dog asks the people, "Have you seen a dog-child with Monkey-Mother?"

"No," they say.

"Do you know where Monkey-Mother lives?"

"No," they say.

Every person or group of people Mrs. Dog meets she asks the same questions and gets the same answers.

Mrs. Dog keeps on going with her traveling and her looking.

Strange fields see Mrs. Dog for the first time.

Mrs. Dog sees people picking coconuts, she questions them. She sees people cutting stems of bananas, she questions them. She comes to an orange grove and sees people picking oranges. She says to the orange-pickers, "Have you seen a dog-child with Monkey-Mother?"

"Yes," they say. "Two days ago. We saw them mango-picking. The dog-child caught the mangoes picked and dropped. Sometimes she

caught them with her hands. Sometimes she went
down onto her hands, kicked up her feet, and
caught the mangoes and put them in the basket."

Anxiously, Mrs. Dog wants to know where the
mango trees are.

The orange-pickers tell her where.

Mrs. Dog finds mango tree after mango tree but
sees nothing of Swing-Swing or Monkey-Mother.

Mrs. Dog goes home.

Mrs. Dog weeps and weeps. Mrs. Dog misses her
first-child oh so much! And Mrs. Dog is tired. Mrs.
Dog and husband and family wonder and wonder,
"What may have happened to our Swing-Swing-
Janey? Eh? Whatever may have happened to our
little Swing-Swing?"

One after the other, everybody remembers how
Janey has many busy antics, and makes them
laugh. They remember how she comes to getting
her name, Swing-Swing, from her father, from her
leaping up to low tree branches and swinging from
one to the next.

Mrs. Dog starts out on her travels again.

A new river sees Mrs. Dog.

She sees men in a canoe, river-fishing. She calls out, "Have you seen a dog-child with Monkey-Mother?"

"Yes," they say. "One hour ago they came back from the other side of the river. The dog-child swam and pulled the raft with Monkey-Mother and family."

Anxiously, Mrs. Dog asks, "Where does she live? Do you know where Monkey-Mother lives?"

"Yes," the men say. And the men explain in detail where Monkey-Mother lives.

Mrs. Dog comes to a rocky barren place. No trees are here. There are only rocks and hills of rocks.

Mrs. Dog stands outside a kind of house of rocks.

Monkey-Mother and children come outside, into the yard.

Monkey-Mother waves her arm around and says, "She's not here. She's not here. Go away. Go away. I tell you—"

Before Monkey-Mother is finished speaking, Swing-Swing comes round some rocks, carrying wood. Monkey-Mother grabs her. She pushes her, bundles her round to the back, and locks her in.

"I want my child," Mrs. Dog shouts. "I want my child!"

Monkey uncles and aunts and cousins all come out waving their arms about, telling Mrs. Dog, "Hop it! Clear off. Get away. And don't you come back!" Oh, the Monkey-people are noisy and threatening!

Mrs. Dog suddenly feels lonely and bullied. Mrs. Dog feels bullied and lonely and hopeless and can't help crying. Mrs. Dog begins to turn away.

The Monkey uncles and aunts and cousins carry on waving about and shouting, repeating, "Hop it! Clear off. Get away. And don't you come back!"

But, you see, just as the fishermen tell Mrs. Dog where Monkey-Mother lives, they also tell Bro Nancy and Bro Dog. So, they arrive!

Listen to the Anancy straightaway,

talking like the best of friendly visitor.

"To Mrs. Monkey-Mother and all, a good-good and abundant afternoon!"

"Good afternoon, Mister Anancy," Monkey-Mother says, in a quiet voice.

Anancy notices everybody has gone quiet and goes on. "I know, there is no need to say, to most respectable strangers, good citizens come to meet good citizens not as a crowd, but in a small-small number of two."

"We are respectable people too, Mister Anancy," Monkey-Mother says.

"That's exactly why none of you can bark? Can any of you bark?" Anancy asks.

"No, sir," Monkey-Mother says.

Anancy knows the moment has come to let Swing-Swing hear him. At the top of his voice, Anancy shouts, "Well—who can bark, let her bark!" Anancy goes on even louder. "Bark now who can bark!"

Swing-Swing-Janey yelps, perhaps forgetting she can bark. Then Swing-Swing begins to bark like wild and crazy, like a terrible hollering in everybody's ears.

Looking badly shamefaced, Monkey-Mother holds her head down.

"Mrs. Monkey-Mother, will you please let out the dog-child and let her come to us?" Anancy commands.

Monkey-Mother says nothing. Monkey-Mother only goes slow-slow and shamefaced and lets out Swing-Swing.

Swing-Swing-Janey comes to her Mother, Mrs. Dog.

Oh, child and mother are happy!

From that time, mothers don't like their children to get too friendly with strangers.

WHEN EMIL GOT HIS HEAD STUCK IN THE SOUP TUREEN

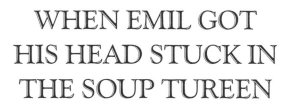

Astrid Lindgren

That day they were having meat broth for dinner in Katthult. Lina had served it up in the flowered soup tureen and they were all sitting around the kitchen table eating soup. Emil especially liked soup; you could hear that when he ate it.

"Must you make that noise?" asked his mother.

"Well, you can't tell you're having soup, otherwise," said Emil.

Everyone had as much as they wanted, and the tureen was empty except for a tiny little drop left at the bottom. But Emil wanted that little drop, and the only way he could get it was by pushing his head into the tureen and sucking it up. And that is just what he did. But just fancy! When he tried to get his head out again he *couldn't*! He was stuck fast. It frightened him and he jumped up from the table and stood there with the tureen like a tub on his head. It came right down over his eyes and ears. He hit at it and screamed. Lina was very upset.

"Our lovely soup tureen," she said. "Our lovely bowl with the flowers on it. Whatever shall we put the soup in now?"

Because although she wasn't very bright, she did realize that while Emil was in the tureen it would be impossible to serve soup in it.

Emil's mother, however, was more worried about Emil.

"Dear sake's alive, how shall we get the child out? We'll have to get the poker and break the bowl."

"Have you taken leave of your senses?" asked Emil's father. "That bowl cost four kronor!"

"Let me have a try," said Alfred, who was a strong, hefty farmhand. He took hold of both handles and lifted the tureen high up in the air—but what good was that? Emil went with it. Because he was stuck really tight. And there he hung, kicking, trying to get back on the ground again.

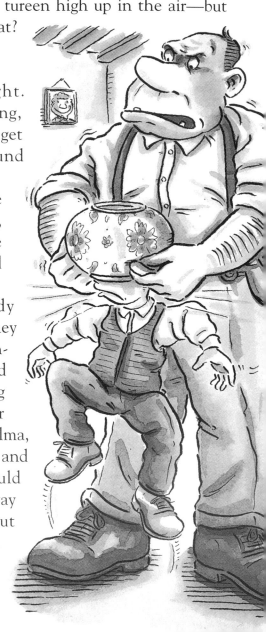

"Let go! Let me get down! Let go, I tell you!" he yelled. So Alfred did let go.

Now everybody was very upset. They stood in the kitchen in a ring around Emil, wondering what to do—father Anton, mother Alma, little Ida, Alfred, and Lina. Nobody could think of a good way of getting Emil out of the soup tureen.

"Look, Emil's crying!" said little Ida, pointing at two big tears sliding down Emil's cheeks from under the edge of the tureen.

"No, I'm not," said Emil. "It's soup."

He sounded as cocky as ever, but it isn't much fun being stuck inside a soup tureen—and supposing he never managed to get out! Poor Emil, when would he be able to wear his cap then?

Emil's mother was in great distress about her little boy. She wanted to take the poker and break the tureen, but his father said, "Not on any account! That bowl cost four kronor. We had better go to the doctor in Mariannelund. He'll be able to get it off. He'll only charge three kronor, and we'll save a krona that way."

Emil's mother thought that a good idea. It isn't every day that one can save a whole krona. Think of all the nice things you could buy with that: perhaps something for little Ida, who would have to stay at home while Emil was out enjoying the trip.

Now all was hurry and bustle in Katthult. Emil must be made tidy; he must be washed and dressed in his best clothes. He couldn't have his hair combed, of course, and nobody could wash his ears, although they certainly needed washing. His mother did try to get her finger under the rim of the soup tureen so as to get at one of Emil's ears, but that wasn't much use for she, too, got stuck in the bowl.

71

"There now!" said little Ida, and father Anton got really angry, though as a rule he was very good-tempered.

"Does anyone else want to get stuck in the tureen?" he shouted. "Well, get on with it for goodness sake, and I'll bring out the big hay wagon and take everyone in the house over to the doctor in Mariannelund."

But Emil's mother wriggled her finger and managed to get it out. "You'll have to go without washing your ears, Emil," she said, blowing her finger. A pleased smile could be seen under the rim of the tureen, and Emil said, "That's the first bit of luck I've had from this tureen."

Alfred had brought the horse and trap to the front steps and Emil now came out to climb into the trap. He was very smart in his striped Sunday suit and black button boots and the soup tureen—of course it did look a trifle unusual, but it was gay and flowery, something like a new-fashioned summer hat. The only criticism that might have been made was that it came down rather too far over Emil's eyes.

Then they set off for Mariannelund.

"Be sure to look after little Ida properly while we're away," called Emil's mother. She sat in front with Emil's father. Emil and the tureen sat at the back, and Emil had his cap beside him on the seat. Because of course he would need something to put on his head for the journey back home. A good job he remembered that!

"What shall I get ready for supper?" shouted Lina, just as the trap was moving off.

"Anything you like," called back Emil's mother. "I've other things to think about just now."

"Well, I'll make meat broth then," said Lina. But at that moment she saw something flowery disappearing around the corner of the road and remembered what had happened. She turned sadly back to Alfred and little Ida.

"It'll have to be black pudding and pork, instead," she said.

Emil had been several times to Mariannelund. He used to like sitting high up in the trap, watching the winding road and looking at the farms they

passed on the way, and the children who lived in them, and the dogs that barked at the gates, and the horses and cows grazing in the meadows. But now it was hardly any fun at all. He sat with a soup tureen over his eyes and could only see a little bit of his own button boots from under the tightly fitting rim of the tureen. He had to keep on asking his father, "Where are we now? Have we got to the pancake place yet? Are we nearly at the pig place?"

Emil had got his own names for all the farms along the road. The pancake place was so-called because of two small, fat children who had once stood by the gate eating pancakes as Emil went past. And the pig place owed its name to a jolly pig whose back Emil would scratch sometimes.

But now he sat gloomily looking down at his own button boots, unable to see either pancakes or jolly little pigs. Small wonder that he kept whining, "Where are we now? Are we nearly at Mariannelund?"

The doctor's waiting room was full of people when Emil and the tureen went striding in. Everybody there was very sorry for him. They realized that an accident had happened. All except one horrid old man who laughed like anything, just as though there was something funny about being stuck in a soup tureen.

"Haha! Haha!" said the old man. "Are your ears cold, my boy?"

"No," said Emil.

"Well, why are you wearing that contraption, then?" asked the old man.

"Because otherwise my ears *would* be cold," said Emil. He too could be funny if he liked, although he was so young.

Then it was his turn to go in and see the doctor, and the doctor didn't laugh at him.

He just said, "Good morning! What are you doing in there?"

Emil couldn't see the doctor, but in spite of that of course he had to greet him, so he bowed as low as he could, tureen and all. Crash! went the tureen, and there it lay, broken in two. For Emil's head had banged against the doctor's desk.

"There goes four kronor up in smoke," said Emil's father to his mother, in a low voice. But the doctor heard him.

"Yes, it's saved you a krona," he said. "Because I generally charge five kronor for getting small boys out of soup tureens, and he's managed to do it all by himself."

THE KING AND THE "K"

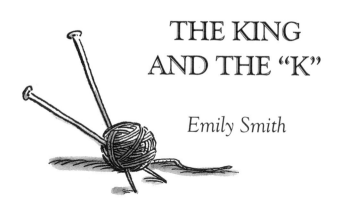

Emily Smith

There was once a small country called Begonia, which was ruled by a young and handsome king. He was a good king and loved by his people. He was also clever, apart from one thing—his spelling. He could spell simple words like "dog" or "log," and slightly more difficult ones like "clog" or "frog," but that was about his limit.

For a long time this did not matter, because the king had a chancellor called Wilbraham, who was a good speller. Wilbraham did all the king's writing for him, and checked his letters and laws and proclamations to make sure there were no silly mistakes.

There came a time, however, when the king decided it was time he got married.

"Begonia needs a queen," he told Wilbraham.

"And I know just the right person—Princess

Irina of Clematis. I hear she is not only very beautiful, but clever, too."

"Yes, Sire," agreed Wilbraham gravely. "The Princess Irina is an excellent choice."

So the king set off for Clematis, with an escort of guards, to ask for Irina's hand.

Now the Princess Irina was indeed both clever and beautiful. She was so clever, in fact, that she had decided she could only marry someone as clever as her—or very nearly, anyway. So she welcomed the king graciously, but explained that before she agreed to marry him, she would have to test him.

"Test me?" said the king in surprise. "Test me on what?"

"Oh, just arithmetic, history, and spelling," said Irina. "Don't worry," she added kindly, "the questions are quite easy."

"Well, all right then," said the king. "I'm ready."

"Arithmetic first," said Irina briskly. "What is ninety-nine plus ninety-nine?"

"One hundred and ninety-eight," said the king promptly.

"A thousand take away one?"

"Nine hundred and ninety-nine."

"Nine times nine?"

"Eighty-one."

"Correct!" said Irina. "Now for history. When was the battle of Freesia?"

T-h-r-o-n-e...

"1172," said the king.

"Who was the first king of Nasturtium?"

"King Iris."

"Who discovered the continent of Chrysanthemum?"

"Sir John Dandelion."

"Excellent," said the princess. "And now for spelling. How do you spell 'throne'?"

Now it so happened that every day the king passed a door in his castle marked THRONE ROOM.

"T–h–r–o–n–e," said the king.

"Good," said Irina. "I told you they were easy questions, didn't I? Now spell 'crown'."

The king had a box in his bedroom marked in big gold letters with the words ROYAL CROWN. So he shut his eyes, thought very hard, and said, "C–r–o–w–n."

"Quite right," said Irina. "Last question now. Can you spell 'knife'?"

Easy, thought the king. "N–i–f–e," he declared confidently.

There was a short silence, and then Irina said, "Oh, dear. You've forgotten the silent 'K' at the beginning." She spoke rather sadly because she would have liked to marry the king. He had nice twinkly eyes.

The king's eyes were not twinkling now, though. He was angry. "Are you telling me," he said slowly, "that you're not going to marry me because of one piffling letter—one 'K' that you can't even hear?"

"I'm afraid so," said Princess Irina. "Otherwise there would be no point in the tests, would there?"

Without another word, the king stalked out of the palace. And such was his rage and disappointment that he didn't speak once all the way home. Back at the castle he summoned Wilbraham.

"One letter wrong!" he raged. "One letter, and I've lost a wife! I must be the laughingstock of Clematis."

"It's an unfortunate outcome certainly, Sire," Wilbraham began, "though not—" but the king burst out again.

"One letter—and what a letter too! A silent 'K'! Silent! It's too absurd! Letters have no right to be silent!"

The king brooded in silence for a moment, and then exclaimed, "I've got it! I know what I'm going to do! I'm going to ban it from the kingdom!"

"Ban what, Sire?" asked the chancellor.

"The silent 'K', of course!"

"Well, I could put the clerk to work at once on

all the books, crossing it out," suggested Wilbraham.

"I don't mean that!" said the king impatiently. "That's not good enough! No, I'm going to get rid of everything with a silent 'K' in it. And that will put paid to that!"

"A bold approach indeed, Sire," said Wilbraham, "but might I suggest—"

"No, Wilbraham!" said the king firmly. "My mind is made up. We'll start with the knives. People will just have to use scissors or choppers or something. They'll find a way. And then . . . what else has a silent 'K' in it?"

Wilbraham considered. "Well, Sire, there's knights, I suppose, and knaves, knobs, knockers, knitting and—" he gave a little cough, "knickers."

"I want the whole lot out of Begonia by the end of the month!" cried the king.

And so a proclamation went up, ordering all the citizens of Begonia to hand in their knives.

All next day people filed up to the castle. They brought carving knives, fish knives, bread knives, butter knives, paring knives, and pruning knives. They brought grand silver knives, humble wooden knives, sharp knives, blunt knives, knives made of gold, brass, bone, ivory, and horn. Housewives brought their kitchen knives, boys brought their whittling knives, and old men brought the knives they used for scraping

out their pipes.

When the very last one had been handed in, the knives were packed into five huge chests and thrown into the castle moat.

"Well, that's done the knives," said the king with satisfaction, as he watched the bubbles. "Now for the knights."

"Well, you can't throw *them* in the moat," said Wilbraham.

"No," said the king. "They'll just have to leave the country."

"But who'll fight dragons and right wrongs and rescue people?" asked Wilbraham.

"Oh, the soldiers can do all that!" said the king.

The knights were ordered to leave Begonia by sunset the following day. A huge crowd gathered to watch—and what a brave sight met their eyes! First to ride off was the Black Knight, the sun shining on his black armor, the plumes nodding on his black helmet. He was followed by the White Knight, the Red Knight, the Brown and the Yellow Knight. (The Yellow Knight was something

of a puzzle as he had never been seen in the land before, nor been known to rescue anyone from anything—not even a cat from the top of a tree.) Their armor chinked and jingled as they rode their proud steeds from the kingdom.

"Good!" said the king, as the last plumes disappeared over the horizon. "Now for the knaves."

So another proclamation went up, ordering all knaves to leave Begonia at once. But the strange thing was that nothing happened at all. No one left. Not even Jim Jakes, who had been in the stocks three times in the last six months.

"The problem is," said Wilbraham, "that no one admits to being a knave."

"Well, it can't be helped for now," said the king. "Let's get on with the knobs and the knockers. I've had an idea about those. We'll do them together."

So right across the land people had to get out their toolboxes. They then took down lion knockers, fish knockers, eagle knockers, pineapple knockers, nice clean shiny knockers, dirty old rusty knockers, knockers that made a good loud bang, and knockers that hardly made any noise at all. As for the knobs . . . they took knobs off walking sticks, wagons, chairs, tables, fences and fireplaces. They removed useful knobs, useless knobs, pretty knobs, ugly knobs, and knobs that people had always banged their heads on.

To set an example, the king walked round the castle pointing out knobs and knockers for the servants to take down. First to go was the huge lion knocker on the castle door. The king himself flung that into the moat.

There was an awkward moment when the king opened his crown box. "Look, Wilbraham," he cried. "Look at those things on my crown! Aren't those knobs?"

"No, Sire," said Wilbraham firmly. "Those are bobbles."

By the end of the day, all the knobs and knockers in the land had been packed into eight cases and dropped into the moat along with the knives.

"The campaign is going well, my good Wilbraham," said the king, pleased. "Tomorrow we shall tackle the knitting."

"Ah," said Wilbraham. "I've been meaning to have a word with you about knitting. The people won't like it. You know how they are about their knitting. They're already grumbling about the knives, the knights, and the knobs and knockers. To take away their knitting will make them furious."

Now, in his heart of hearts, the king knew Wilbraham was right. The people of Begonia loved knitting—all of them. Children learned to knit as soon as they could hold the needles, teenagers knitted, courting couples knitted, mothers and fathers, grandparents and great-grandparents knitted. Lords and laborers knitted, so did merchants and milkmaids, soldiers and sailors, teachers and tinkers. Even Jim Jakes had once knitted a shawl for his mother. They knitted all the things you can think of, and some you can't. They would have knitted chairs and books and bottles if they could.

The king knew this quite well, but he just would not listen to reason.

"I'm sorry, Wilbraham, but it can't be helped. They'll have to weave or sew or crochet instead. And if anyone is caught knitting, I shall fine them ten gold pieces."

The proclamation went out that afternoon, and then indeed there were angry faces across the land. But no one wanted to be fined ten gold pieces, so they all handed over their knitting needles and knitting patterns when the soldiers called.

The next fine day, the king rode round his kingdom to survey his lands. Usually when he did this, he was greeted in every village by smiling and cheering crowds. But this time there was no such welcome. As he and his guards rode in, backs were turned, shutters were closed, and doors were slammed.

Late in the day the royal party crossed a meadow. In the meadow was a flock of geese, and minding the geese was a young goose-girl. The goose-girl was sitting against a tree and—the king couldn't believe his eyes—she was knitting.

He reined in his horse. "Bring that girl over here!" he ordered his men.

When the goose-girl arrived, she dropped a curtsey and said, "Your Majesty?"

"What do you mean by knitting?" the king demanded angrily. "Don't you know there's a proclamation banning all knitting in the kingdom?"

"Yes, I do," said the goose-girl. "But I'm knitting some bedsocks for my grandmother. She needs them, for her feet get very cold at night."

"Do you place your grandmother's feet over a royal proclamation?" asked the king sternly.

"Well, I do over that one. It's so silly," said the goose-girl, and everyone gasped.

"Shall we tie her up and take her back to the castle, Sire?" asked a guard.

"No," said the king. "Not yet, anyway. Tell me, girl. Why do you think it's silly?"

"Well, Your Majesty, I understand you want to rid the kingdom of everything beginning with a silent 'K'."

"Yes," said the king. "That's right."

"If you do that, you will bring ruin and misery on your land."

"Oh?" said the king. "And why is that?"

"Because then you will rid the country of all knowledge. And where would men and women be without knowledge?"

"Hmmm," said the king. "But is knowledge really so useful? Look at me. I'm king of all this land, but I can't even spell 'knife'."

"Oh, *spelling*," said the goose-girl. "I'm not talking about that sort of knowledge. I'm talking about *real* knowledge—knowing good from evil, truth from lies, knowing who to trust and who to fear, knowing when to speak and when to be silent, knowing when to act—and when to pass by."

There was silence. And then the king spoke again, in a more kindly voice than before. "But you know, my dear, you disobeyed a royal proclamation. You will have to pay ten gold pieces."

"I haven't got ten gold pieces," said the goose-girl.

"In that case, come to the castle tomorrow, and I will choose one of your geese instead. And be sure to be there," warned the king. "Otherwise you could go to prison."

The next day, the king was woken by a fanfare of trumpets. He quickly got dressed and ran downstairs to find a herald with a message from Princess Irina.

"I come bearing good news from her Royal Highness, the Princess Irina of Clematis," announced the herald. "The princess, in her great kindness, has reconsidered your proposal of marriage. She has graciously decided to accept your suit—even though you can't spell 'knife'."

"Hmmm," said the king, and the next moment in walked the goose-girl followed by her flock of geese.

"I've come to give you one of my geese," said the goose-girl.

"Well, I don't want one," said the king.

"Oh!" said the goose-girl, and she began to feel a bit frightened. Would she have to go to prison?

"I don't want you to give me a goose. I want you to give me your hand and be my queen," said the king. He looked into her green eyes. "Will you?" he asked.

"Yes," said the goose-girl. "I will marry you if you stop this silly campaign against the silent 'K'."

"Of course!" said the king. "I was going to do that anyway."

He turned to the herald. "Go back to Clematis," he said, "and tell your princess she's caused a lot of bother in this country and I'm not going to marry her. She may think she's clever, but I think this young lady here is ten times as clever, and I'm going to marry her instead!"

The herald was very surprised, but did as he was told. When he got home and delivered the king's message, Princess Irina flew into a rage and

boxed the poor man's ears. She was last heard of married to a lawyer.

Back in Begonia, everyone was overjoyed that the king had come to his senses at last. The credit for this went to the goose-girl, and they welcomed her straightaway as their queen. A good wife, they reckoned, is one who can stop her husband being silly.

Wilbraham was especially pleased to see the end of the silent "K" campaign. He had been getting very worried about what would happen when the king got round to "knickers."

The knives, knobs, and knockers were dragged up from the bottom of the moat. They were found to be hardly damaged at all, and returned to their owners. So were the knitting needles and the patterns. The king sent the knights a polite letter (written by Wilbraham), asking them to come back, which they did.

The royal couple had two children, a son and a daughter. Wilbraham made sure they both learned to spell from an early age. The little prince was never much better than his father, though, and always spelt "gnome" without the "G."

To this day there's no knocker on the castle door (you have to bang with a stick or shout). The door is kept like that to remind everyone of the time the king waged his campaign against the silent "K."

WHEN GRANDMA TOOK A BACK SEAT

Nancy Blishen

It was Christmas Eve, and Tom and Kate were very excited—over-excited, their mother said. But then Grandma and Grandpa had come to stay, and the thought of bulging stockings on Christmas morning; the Christmas tree with the parcels round it; and all those good things to eat, made it difficult to sit still.

"There's a bowl of icing on the kitchen table, ready for the Christmas cake. I bet you daren't go in while Mum's not there and take a bit," Tom whispered to his sister.

Now if there was one thing that made Kate furious with her brother—especially as he was only eight, two years younger than her—it was to be told she daren't do something. So, giving him a withering look, she slipped into the kitchen and put her finger first in the bowl, and then in her mouth. It happened to be just the moment when her mother came back.

"Katie!"

Kate went red and nearly choked on the icing.

"B-But it tastes so much better when you steal a bit than it does on the cake," she said.

To her surprise, her mother burst out laughing. "That's exactly what I used to say to *my* mother when I was your age. You're forgiven this time! And Tom! You can come out from behind the door. Here's a bit of icing for you too, though you don't deserve it. And now will you *please* go back into the living room."

It was then that Grandma came to the rescue.

"Katie, if you go up to my room you'll find a brown paper bag on the bedside table. Bring it down to the living room. And Tom, fetch your penknife. Then we'll need the little shovel that stands in the hearth."

The children were intrigued. Gran always had good ideas, but they couldn't imagine how this one was going to turn out. What could be done with a brown paper bag, a penknife, and a little shovel?

When they were settled on the couch in front of the fire, Grandma opened the bag and took out a big handful of chestnuts. With Tom's knife she split the skins; then she put the nuts on the shovel and carefully placed it on top of the hottest coals in the fire.

"Oh goodie! Roast chestnuts!" cried Kate. "Did you have them at Christmas when you were a little girl, Gran!"

"Yes," said Gran. "That was just one of the treats we looked forward to. When I was small we had chestnuts—*and* oranges and bananas and dates—only at Christmas. They weren't in the shops the rest of the year."

"Was Christmas exciting . . . in those days?" asked Tom.

"Oh yes. And I remember one year that was even more exciting than usual . . ."

There seemed to be a story coming.

"Tell us about it."

"It was Boxing Day. We'd had a wonderful Christmas with my grandparents. It had been snowing heavily all day, and my father thought we should start for home: it began to get dark quite early in the afternoon."

"You had a car?" asked Kate.

"Yes, we did. But it wasn't a bit like the cars you have today. It was very small, only big enough for two people, and it had a hood that folded down, like the hood on a pram."

"But if there was only room for two," said Tom, "where did you sit?"

"In the dickey seat."

"Dickey seat?" cried Kate and Tom together.

"You know where today cars have a boot at the back? Well, we had a flap which lifted up. Under it was a padded seat, and the flap itself was padded underneath, too, so there was something to lean back on. Do you see? Of course, it meant my mum and dad were under cover, under the hood, while I was out in the open, because the hood didn't cover the dickey seat. But I never minded. I wore lots of warm clothes, and I was tucked in with a rug. When it was really cold, as it was that Christmas, I hugged a hot water bottle."

"Grandma, something's burning!" shouted Tom.

"Oh, the chestnuts! Quick!" Grandma took the

shovel off the fire. They had to bounce a chestnut
from one hand to the other until it cooled enough
to hold; then the skins came off easily to reveal
the edible bits inside, browned and hot and
delicious. There was nothing for several minutes
but the sound of munching. Then, her mouth full,
Kate said:

"Please go on with the story, Gran."

Fortunately, Gran's mouth was a bit emptier.
"We started to drive home through the snow.
It was all right at first, but then a white wall rose
up in front of us. There was a whooshing sound,

the bonnet of the car disappeared, and we stopped. We'd driven into a snowdrift. In those days, you see, there were no snowplows, and the wind sometimes blew the snow into piles so high you couldn't see over the top. The car wouldn't go forward and it wouldn't go back, and my dad didn't know what to do. I remember my mum was so worried that she cried a little, but I thought it was a great adventure, and I wanted to giggle."

"Whatever did you do?" asked Tom.

"Suddenly we saw lights coming toward us on the other side of the road. It was a bus. When the driver saw us, he stopped and got down from his cab. He scratched his head and joked: 'What's this then? Playing Santa Claus, are you, in his sledge? Where are the reindeer? Under the snow?'

"My dad didn't think it was at all funny, but this

time I really had to giggle. The driver went back
to his bus and called, 'Everybody out!' and the passengers—there were ten or twelve of them— all
climbed down into the snow.

"'Now,' said the driver. 'This is such a small,
light car, I think if we all give a tug and a heave
it'll be out of that snowdrift in no time.' So that's
what they did! They pushed and tugged us free.
And then—this is the amazing bit—they half-slid,
half-lifted the car sideways into the wheel tracks
the bus had made. And there we were, on the
wrong side of the road."

"'Right,' said the bus driver, 'I reckon you'll be
fine for the next six or seven miles, keeping in the
tracks we've made. That's as far as I've come.'

"'Perfect,' said my dad, 'because that's as far as
we have to go.'

"And I remember all the passengers cheered, and we thanked them and the bus driver, and we started on our way."

"Hang on a minute, Gran," said Tom. "What happened when you met all the other cars coming toward you? I mean, you were on the wrong side of the road."

"Very few people drove at all in the winter—hardly any in bad weather—so, believe it or not, Tom, we didn't meet a single car. Six miles of nobody."

There was a call from the kitchen. Grandpa and Dad were back: it was time for supper.

"You'll tell us another story tomorrow, Gran?" asked Kate.

"If there's time," said Grandma. But she smiled secretly to herself. She knew what Grandpa and Dad had been out for, what they'd brought home and hidden in the garage. There was a red bike for Tom and a silver bike for Kate. Grandma couldn't help feeling that tomorrow there wouldn't be much time for storytelling.

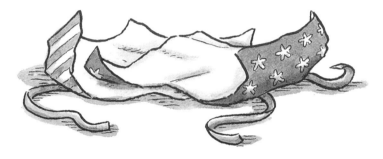

MOVING DAY

Traditional Iroquois Tale
retold by Roger Squire

Turtle forced his eyes open and thrust his head slowly out from his shell to see whether the night had been cold enough to rim his pond with frost. The Earth, he found, was still untouched. The sun was late and weak, however, and the brook murmured drowsily as it tumbled over the last bed of rock before reaching the pond. It was time to be thinking about his long winter's sleep.

Suddenly he was no longer content with his way of life. Why did he have to crawl into the mud each fall and stay there till spring, locked in a silent prison? Why couldn't he have a winter home as nice as some of his friends?

There was Squirrel, for example. What a wonderful nest he had high in the butternut tree! Inside its leafy walls he was safe and comfortable, with enough room to move around in as well.

Turtle decided that when the sun had warmed him a little, he would ask Squirrel to help him build as pleasant a home upon the ground.

He found his friend clinging to the far end of a branch with his wife scolding him from the other.

"May I ask you about a problem?" Turtle said.

"Gladly!" Squirrel replied. "Gladly!" He jumped to another tree and ran down its trunk.

"And don't you dare go off anywhere without fixing it!" his wife called after him.

"What's the trouble?" Turtle asked with sympathy.

"She says I didn't build our house right and she has a stiff neck from the draft!" Squirrel grumbled. "I wish she had a stiff jaw too! Then she couldn't complain so much! What's wrong with you?"

"I was just wishing that I had a winter home like yours," Turtle admitted. "But I guess yours isn't perfect, either."

"Far from it!" Squirrel exclaimed. "My wife and I

can't get away from each other! If I had a nice big house like Raccoon's, I could live inside one branch and my wife inside another. I could store my seeds and nuts in it, too, so I wouldn't have to go out in the cold to get something to eat!"

"If Raccoon should give it up for any reason," Turtle said, "why couldn't you live in the branches and I live down among the roots?"

Then they looked at each other and smiled.

"If I had your brain," Squirrel said, "I could find a reason why he should give it to us."

"And if I had your gift of speech," Turtle told him, "I would know how to talk him into it."

"Then let's work together," Squirrel suggested, "and see what we can do."

"Fine!" said Turtle. "That tree doesn't look very safe to me."

Squirrel laughed. "I'll make him think it's going to fall over tomorrow!" he said.

So off they went that evening to the old maple in which Raccoon lived the year round. It was a splendid home for anyone, with three hollow branches and a huge, partly hollow trunk.

"Good evening," Squirrel called.

Raccoon, who had just awakened, looked out of his window. "Welcome!" he exclaimed. He thought that Squirrel was his friend. Besides, he was as polite as he was tidy. "Welcome to you both!"

"Your house is what we want to talk to you about," Squirrel explained. "Turtle is so worried that he asked me to come over and see you."

Raccoon studied both Squirrel and Turtle carefully. He was wiser than they thought. He could have been chief of all the raccoons if he had wanted to. Surely they didn't know that only last night he had found a dangerous crack on the thin side of the trunk and had picked out a new home? He decided that they were up to something. He decided to play as innocent as they.

"I'm very grateful for your interest," he said to Turtle. "What do you think is wrong with it?"

"Don't you know," Squirrel said, "that Bear chose this tree as his home but never moved in because he was sure that it would be blown down by the first bad winter wind?"

Raccoon pretended to be worried. "No," he said. "He didn't tell me that."

"Why don't you let me examine the different parts," Squirrel offered, "and find out whether it's safe?"

Raccoon remembered that the crack did not show through the bark. "The children are still asleep," he said. "But if you could do it from the outside, that would be fine, although I'm afraid I can't pay you very much."

This was a new thought to Squirrel. He had not expected to be paid. But what harm would it do to earn a little present by his trickery, as well as a new home?

"Oh, I wouldn't demand a payment from a friend," he said. "But of course it will take a lot of time and careful thought. So if you happen to know where you could get—let's say, about twenty walnuts or hickory nuts, it would keep my wife a little quieter."

Raccoon did happen to know where there were twenty walnuts—right in one of Squirrel's own hiding places, which he had discovered by accident three days ago. And he saw no reason why he should pay Squirrel to look at a house which he was going to give up.

"Very well," he answered. "I'll deliver that number of walnuts when you have finished the job."

Squirrel leaped up onto a stump happily.

Then he studied Raccoon's tree from its crown to its roots, jerking his tail up and down as he did when he was excited. "I certainly didn't think it was that bad!" he exclaimed.

"Bad in what way?" Raccoon asked.

"Look at it!" Squirrel exclaimed. "It even leans toward the south. So when the north wind blows, it already has a head start to the ground."

"Oh, dear!" said Raccoon. "And it has such lovely storage space."

Squirrel climbed down solemnly. "I'll do what repair work I can," he offered, "so it won't fall down right away. But I can't promise anything without charging you more nuts."

"If I could get some help," Raccoon asked, "wouldn't it be much safer to move?"

At this Squirrel almost laughed out loud, "It might be," he agreed. "Yes, it might. But where will you get the help?"

Raccoon was pretty sure that Squirrel had stored other pockets of nuts near the first one. So he made a new offer.

"I know a tree that might do," he said. "But I want a separate nest for every member of the family. Your teeth are sharper than mine. I'll give you twice the number of walnuts if you'll chew the nests out for me."

"I think I could," said Squirrel happily.

"And it would be much easier to do," Raccoon said, "if someone would take care of the children while my wife and I are making the beds more comfortable with grass and ferns."

"I will make the new rooms," Squirrel said. "And Turtle and I will take turns watching the babies."

Then Squirrel and Turtle said good-bye and left. All three were pleased with the bargain.

Turtle, however, was not quite as pleased as Squirrel. "What good will twenty nuts do me?" he asked. "Why didn't you demand ten nuts and ten fish?"

"Because I'm doing most of the work," Squirrel said, "and I don't like fish."

"You *should* do most of the work!" Turtle pointed out. "You will have most of the tree!"

"Let's not quarrel," Squirrel said. "We're both going to have a wonderful home for the winter."

Squirrel did not love his work. Even with his sharp teeth, it was hard to cut out four nests from living wood. And, of course, his wife scolded him for being away so much. How glad he would be when the cold weather slowed down her tongue!

Raccoon, on the other hand, was so pleased that he dug up half of Squirrel's nuts and paid him these before he was through. Then he watched where Squirrel hid them and dug them up again for his second payment . . .

Then suddenly the north wind began to moan in the distance, and came down out of the hills, fleeing before the frost spirits. "Hurry, hurry, hurry!" it moaned. "It's cold, cold, cold!"

Raccoon did not have to hurry. He was settled now in a nice warm new home, paid for in full.

Squirrel thought that he too did not have to hurry.

"Now I will show you what I have been working at," he said to his wife. "You'll be sorry that you scolded me when you see our new home." With a nut in his mouth, he led her from branch to branch toward the Raccoon's tree, which was now vacant and ready to be lived in.

They had barely started, however, when they heard a great crash in its direction.

"What was that?" his wife asked.

"It sounded like a tree," he said in a voice quiet with fear.

They went on. They jumped from rock to rock across a narrow brook. They climbed a trunk to their natural paths again. Squirrel dreaded to look down. Then all too soon there was Raccoon's tree, twisted and broken, lying on the ground. Beside it lay Turtle, stunned.

"That's probably the tree we just heard," Squirrel's wife said. "Don't stop here! We must go on to our new home."

Squirrel turned about unhappily and headed back toward their nest. "That was our new home!" he said. "We'll have to sleep close together tonight to keep warm."

It is better to forget what his wife said.

And Turtle? He had lived a long time and knew that life held many disappointments. He recovered from the shock and went back to his pond. There he dug his way slowly into the mud.

The winter might be long. But at least he would pass it in peace.

A
NARROW
SQUEAK

Dick King-Smith

"Do you realize," said Ethel, "that tomorrow is our Silver Wedding Day?"

"So soon?" said Hedley in a surprised voice. "How time flies! Why, it seems but yesterday that we were married."

"Well, it isn't," said Ethel sharply. "You only have to look at me to see that."

Hedley looked at her.

She seems to have put on a great deal of weight, he thought. Not that she isn't still by far the most beautiful mouse in the world, of course, but there's a lot more of her now.

"You have certainly grown," he said tactfully.

"Grown?" snapped Ethel. "And whose fault is that, pray? Anyone would think you didn't know why I'm blown out like a balloon. Goodness knows what sort of a father you will make."

"A father?" said Hedley. "You mean . . . ?"

"Any time now," said Ethel. "And I'm starving hungry, Hedley. Fetch us something nice to eat, do. I could just fancy something savory."

She sighed deeply as her husband hurried away. Was there ever such a mouse, she said to herself. So handsome, but so *thick*. Let's hope he doesn't walk straight down the cat's throat. I wouldn't put it past him and then there won't be any Silver Wedding.

A mouse's life is, of course, a short one, fraught with hazards. For those that survive their childhood, Death looms in many shapes and forms, among them the cat, the poison bait and the trap, and mice have learned to commemorate anniversaries in good time. "Better early than never" is a favorite mouse proverb, and Ethel and Hedley's Silver Wedding was to be celebrated twenty-five days after their marriage.

If they were lucky, they would go on to a Pearl, a Ruby, a Golden, and, should they be spared to enjoy roughly two months of wedded bliss, to a Diamond Wedding Anniversary. Beyond that, no sensible mouse cared to think.

If only Hedley was more sensible, Ethel thought as she lay, uncomfortably on account of the pressure within her, in her nest. Not that he isn't still by far the most beautiful mouse in the world, of course, but he's so accident-prone.

Hardly a day passed when Ethel did not hear, somewhere about the house, a thin cry of alarm, indicating that Hedley had just had a narrow squeak.

He goes about in a dream, she said to herself. He doesn't think. Surely other mice didn't stand in the path of vacuum cleaners, or explore inside tumble driers, or come close to drowning in a bowl of cat's milk?

In fact, Hedley was thinking quite hard as he emerged from the hole in the skirting board that

was the entrance to their home, and prepared to make his way across the kitchen floor.

"A father!" he murmured happily to himself. "I am to be a father! And soon! How many children will there be, I wonder? How many will be boys, how many girls? And what shall we call them? What fun it will be, choosing the names!"

This was what Ethel had meant when she said that Hedley did not think. Her thoughts were very practical and filled with common sense, and she was quick to make up her mind. By contrast, Hedley was a daydreamer and much inclined to be absentminded when, as now, he was following up an idea.

He had just decided to call his eldest son Granville after a favorite uncle, when he bumped into something soft and furry, something that smelled, now that he came to think of it, distinctly unpleasant.

The cat, fast asleep in front of the Aga cooker, did not wake, but it twitched its tail.

With a shrill cry, Hedley ran for cover. The larder door was ajar, and he slipped in and hid behind a packet of cornflakes.

The noise he had made reached Ethel's ears, and filled her mind, as so often over the previous twenty-four days, with thoughts of widowhood. It also woke the cat, who rose, stretched and padded toward the larder.

"Not in there, puss!" said its owner, coming into her kitchen, and she shut the larder door.

Hedley was a prisoner.

For some time he crouched motionless. As happened after such frights, his mind was a blank. But gradually his thoughts returned to those unborn children. The eldest girl, now—what was she to be called?

After a while Hedley decided upon Dulcibel, his grandmother's name. But then suppose Ethel did not agree? Thinking of Ethel reminded him of her last words. "Fetch us something nice to eat, do," she had said. "I could just fancy something savory."

Hedley raised his snout and sniffed.

This little room, in which he had never been before, certainly smelled of all kinds of food, and this reminded him that he was himself a bit peckish. He began to explore the larder, climbing up onto its shelves and running about to see what he could find. I'll have a snack, he said to himself, to keep me going, and then I'll find something really nice to take back to Ethel.

Much of the food in the larder was in cans or packets, but Hedley found a slab of fruit cake and some butter in a dish and a plate of cold chips. At last, feeling full, he hid behind a row of tins and settled down for a nap.

Meanwhile, back at the nest, Ethel was growing increasingly uneasy. He must have had his chips, she thought, and our children will be born fatherless. She was hungry, she was uncomfortable, and she was more and more worried that Hedley had not returned.

"Oh Hedley, how I shall miss you!" she breathed. "*So* handsome, but so *thick*."

While Hedley was sleeping off his huge meal, the larder door was opened.

"Just look at this cake!" a woman's voice said. "And these leftover chips! And the butter—little footmarks all over it! We've got mice."

"Put the cat in there," said a man's voice.

"Can't do that or it'll be helping itself too."

"Well, set a trap then. And put some poison down."

And a little later, the larder door was closed again.

Hedley slept the whole night through. He dreamed of happy times to come. In his dream, his handsome sons and his beautiful daughters had grown old enough to leave the nest, and he was taking them on a conducted tour of the house. Then boldly he led them all, Granville and Dulcibel and the rest, and their mother too, through the cat flap and out into the garden.

"For we will picnic," he said to them, "in the strawberry bed. The fruit is ripe and the weather exceedingly pleasant."

"Oh Papa!" the children cried. "What fun that will be!"

"But are you not afraid of the cat, Hedley dear?" said Ethel nervously.

"Ethel, Ethel," said Hedley. "When have you ever known me afraid of anything?" and the children chorused, "Oh, brave Papa!". . .

He woke from his dream with a number of other possible names for the impending family in mind— Eugene, Tallulah, Hereward, and Morwenna were four that he particularly fancied —when he suddenly remembered with a sharp pang of guilt that Ethel was still unfed.

I shall get the rough edge of her tongue, he

thought, and he looked about for a tasty item of food, small enough for him to carry.

He climbed down to a lower shelf and found something which had not, he was sure, been there before.

It was a saucer containing a number of little blue pellets, and beside it there was an opened packet. Had Hedley been able to read, he would have seen that on the packet was written:

MOUSE POISON, KEEP AWAY FROM
DOMESTIC ANIMALS

At it was, thinking how unusual and attractive the blue pellets looked, he took a mouthful of them. She'll love these, he thought, such a pretty color, and he ran down to the floor of the larder only to find the door shut. Bother, thought Hedley. How am I to get out of this place?

He was considering this problem in a half-hearted way, for part of his mind was still occupied with names—would Annabel be better than Morwenna?—when his nose caught a most exciting smell. It was cheese, a little square lump of it, conveniently placed on a low shelf.

The cheese was in fact on a little wooden platform, an odd-looking thing that had a metal arm and a spring attached to it, but Hedley, busy deciding that after all he preferred Morwenna, did not stop to think about this. It's Ethel's favorite food, he said to himself, and just the right size for me to carry back, and he spat out the little blue pellets and ran to grab the cheese.

Whether it was his speed or whether the trap had not been lightly enough set, Hedley got away with it.

SNAP! went the trap, missing him (though not by a whisker for it cut off three of them), and Hedley gave, through his mouthful of cheese, a muffled squeak of fright.

"Listen!" said the woman's voice, and "You got him!" said the man's, and the larder door was opened.

For once Hedley did not daydream. He streaked across the kitchen floor and into his hole, the lump of cheese clenched in his jaws.

Ethel regarded him silently from the nest.

Hedley dropped his burden before her.

"Sorry I'm late," he panted. "I got held up. Here, it's Farmhouse Cheddar, your favorite. How have you been?"

"Busy," said Ethel shortly.

"Busy?" said Hedley.

"Yes," said Ethel.

She attacked the cheese hungrily, while Hedley lay and got his breath back. Funny, he thought, she looks slimmer than she did yesterday. As slim, in fact, as the day we met, and what a meeting that was! I remember it as though it were yesterday . . .

"Hedley!" said Ethel now, licking her lips as she finished the cheese. "You do know what day it is, don't you?"

"Wednesday, I think," said Hedley. "Or it may be Thursday. I'm not sure."

"Hedley," said Ethel. "It is our Silver Wedding Day."

"Oh!" cried Hedley. "I quite forgot."

Typical, thought Ethel. He'd forget his head if it wasn't screwed on.

"I have a present for you," she said, and she rose and stood aside from the nest.

In the middle of a comfortable, warm bed, made out of flock from a chair lining, and feathers from an eiderdown, and a mass of newspaper scraps, lay six fat, pink, naked babies.

"Three boys and three girls," she said. "Neat, eh?"

Oh! thought Hedley. What could be neater! Granville and Dulcibel, Eugene and Tallulah, and Hereward and Morwenna.

"Oh, Ethel dearest," he said. "I have no present for you but my love."

At these words Ethel's annoyance melted away. What a fine-looking mouse he still is, she thought, not a gray hair on him. In fact, he looks no older than he did at our wedding, twenty-five long days ago.

Hedley sat in a daze, gazing at the babies.

Then he said. "Oh, Ethel! To think that you did this all on your own! You're so clever!"

And you're so *thick*, thought Ethel fondly, but out loud she said, "Oh Hedley, you are *so* handsome!"

A BARREL OF CHICKEN

Robert Newton Peck

"You're afraid," said Soup.

"No, I'm not."

"Then what are you just standing there for?"

"Well, it looks like kind of a steep hill. Maybe we should try it on the level."

"I knew you'd be scared."

"I ain't scared."

"Then why don't you get inside the barrel?"

"Here's why," I said, showing Soup a bent nail inside the old apple barrel.

"It's just an old nail."

"Yeah, but if it rips my sweater, my mother won't like it."

My mother already took notice that I look worse when I come home from school than when I start out. I never see a difference, but she always does.

"You're afraid."

"I'm not afraid of rolling down Dugan's Hill in a barrel. Just afraid of tearing a rip to the sweater."

"What do you care?" said Soup. "After all, it's my sweater."

"Used to be," I said. "Your mother gave it to my mother for some of us to wear. Reckon it's my sweater now, since you outgrowed it."

"That's because," said Soup as he gave me a punch on my arm for emphasis, "I'm bigger 'n you. I can't even get into that old sweater."

"And I can't get into that old barrel."

Soup looked around for a rock and found one. Rolling the barrel so the nail was against the ground, he pounded it flat against the raw, splintery wood.

"There," said Soup, "I fixed the nail."

With a doubtful eye, I got down on my hands and knees to inspect the barrel's newly improved interior. I noticed then that some of the staves were rotten and loose.

"Get in," said Soup.

I started to back into the barrel, feet first, taking one last look down the full length of Dugan's Hill. I backed in only an inch or two, until I felt Soup's restraining hand tug on my belt.

"Head first," said Soup, "not feet first."

"How come?" I said, happily exiting on my hands and knees.

"Because," said Soup.

I knew better than to ask Soup "because what?" As far as Soup was concerned, his one-word explanation—because—was enough for me. It would be a waste of good time to offer further documentation for his decision that proper barrel-entering was performed head first. Argument would now be useless. Soup never made a moot point. And so with a sigh of resignation, Soup's sweater and I occupied the barrel in the approved manner.

The barrel, prior to my entry—or rather reentry—had been light inside. Now that I filled it, it seemed dark. To make matters worse, the inside bottom of the old apple barrel that I now faced still carried a few overripe remains of its recently emptied cargo.

"You see?" said Soup, "now when you roll inside the barrel, nothing can hit your face. There's a reason for everything."

I was about to add, "Nothing can hit my face except rotten apples." But I didn't. It would be folly to talk back to Luther Wesley Vinson when your rear end is pointed shoe-level in his direction and within his range, especially in such an undefended position. You had to know in this world when to keep your mouth shut and your behind inconspicuous.

"Ready?" said Soup.

"Ready." I really wasn't ready at all, not prepared in the least. But what good would it do to say I wasn't?

"Now," said Soup, turning the barrel with precision, "make sure you stay on the road. 'Cause if'n you don't, you'll roll off down the meadow and through a fence into Biscardi's hen coop."

"I will?"

"Not if you stay on the road," Soup said.

"How do I do that?"

"Rob, don't you know anything about rolling in a barrel? Any jackass can do it."

"That's me," I said. "I'm in there somewhere."

"Remember this one thing," said Soup, his voice assuming his I-know-and-you-don't attitude, rather like Miss Kelly. No one ever questioned Miss Kelly. Her words were dipped in bronze.

"Remember to keep your weight even in the barrel. The important thing is balance," said Soup.

"Balance," I said in a hollow voice, as if it came

from deep inside a barrel. It did.

"Brace yourself," said Soup. "And don't tear my sweater. I may want it back."

"No, you won't. It's got apple on it."

"You'll go on the count of three," said Soup.

"Why three?"

"That's the way you do it. As I holler out the number, you're supposed to say the same number. Okay? One!"

"One," I said.

"Two!"

"Two."

"THREE!"

On the final number, I never got a chance to answer. Soup gave the barrel a heck of a push and also what sounded and felt like an extra kick, to insure I reached maximum rolling speed. Soup was a perfectionist in so many wondrous ways.

Down we went; the barrel, Soup's sweater, and I—down Dugan's Hill. I put fear out of my mind in order to concentrate on balance. Faster and faster the barrel rolled, so fast that some of it came apart. Around and around I went; my head was spinning, and I forgot what little I knew on the topic of balance. I did try to brace myself, but it didn't really matter anymore. When you walk *up* Dugan's Hill, you're not fully aware of its many and countless bumps. Yet rolling down it inside an apple barrel, each bump seems to make itself known.

Around and around, faster and faster and faster the barrel rolled. I figured there had to be *some* fun to it; and yet my mind seemed to be asking: when would the fun start? I tried to tell myself that it was great sport.

It didn't work. It wasn't fun. There was no joy to it at all. Not one bit. It hurt, it was scary, it made you so dizzy and weak that you wanted to cry, scream, and throw up all at the same time.

And you got wood slivers in your hands.

Some people might call this fun. I sure don't.

There was a loud noise, and then another. It sounded like a barrel with a fool in it, going at great speed, smashing through the side of Biscardi's chicken coop. I was thrown out of the barrel, but still moving, rolling, and sliding through a thick and slippery carpet of straw and hen manure. My last thought, as I slid into a hysterical group of Plymouth Rock matrons, as if they had been second base, was of Soup's sweater.

I'd have to be careful, I thought, as I tried to slow myself down by grabbing a chicken, or I'd really do more damage to the sweater than just a little old nail hole. Several staves out of the barrel and a rusty hoop seemed to be sliding along with me. It sure was a long hen house.

There was another crash, a chorus of excited cackles, and one very angry yell as I finally came to a stop just as Mrs. Biscardi dropped the eggs.

My first thought, as I lay on the floor of the chicken coop and looked up at Mrs. Biscardi with broken eggs dripping from all ten of her fingers, was that I hoped I didn't get any yellowy egg stuff on the sweater. Soup was a regular guy, but he could be right fussy about certain matters that concerned his property, both present and past. I put my hands on my chest to feel if the sweater was still in one piece.

All I felt was my shirt and part of an eggshell. To my dismay, I wasn't even wearing a sweater.

And yet my arms were wearing a sweater and so was my neck. I was about to Mrs. Biscardi if she'd seen a brown wool sweater, but I decided she had

other things on her mind. One thing that seemed
to occupy her thoughts was a large, gaping hole in
the side of her chicken coop. The hole itself
wasn't so bad. The real problem was that most of

the hens were running out through the hole and down the road.

I looked through the hole for Soup. No sign of him. Soup had evaporated as mysteriously as had most of his sweater. Mrs. Biscardi seemed to be even more emotional than even her most excited hen. There was at least a dozen hens flapping around and cackling their heads off. The air was a snowstorm of chicken feathers, and so was the inside of my mouth. Mrs. Biscardi was saying things to either me or the escaping hens, and they didn't sound very friendly. But seeing neither the chickens nor I could understand even one word of Italian, none of us really took offense at the remarks that seemed to tumble from her lips without so much as a breath in between.

Mrs. Biscardi was dreadfully upset over something. She was so busy trying to guard the hole and trying to catch six or seven screaming chickens at once, while holding one hen firmly between her chubby knees, that it seemed to be an excellent time for me to scram. Getting to my feet, I ran out of the chicken-wire door. A piece of brown yarn was around my neck and I gave it a yank, but it didn't come loose. As I ran around to the other side of the hen coop, more yarn caught my eye. It was a long piece of yarn, starting from inside the hen house and stretching straight up Dugan's Hill.

I climbed the hill, following the strand of yarn as I retraced the route that I had rolled inside the apple barrel only a minute earlier. The yarn came to an end, snagged around a rotted barrel stave and wound around a nail.

It's not easy to believe how anyone could walk home smelling of rotten apple, broken egg, and chicken manure and be as happy as I was. I even whistled, despite the licking I'd probably get for the mess I'd turned myself into. But now I was a full-fledged member of that brave and fearless group of adventurers who had the courage to roll down Dugan's Hill in a barrel.

In my pocket was a large wad of brown yarn. So if Soup wanted his sweater back, I'd give it to him.

But he'd have to knit it all over again.

THE KING WHO WAS FRIED

Edward Blishen

Have you ever heard of this king who vowed he'd not eat a crumb of bread on any day of the week, nor take even a single sip from a glass of water, until he'd given twenty pounds of gold away to the poor?

Couldn't be done, you say. Twenty pounds of gold multiplied by 365 for the days of the year (or 366 for a leap year) equals . . . an enormous amount of gold. Say it went on for ten years. An enormous amount of gold multiplied by ten is . . . an absolutely breathtaking amount of gold. Couldn't be done. No king could ever be that rich.

Well, listen to this. Day after day, before King Karan—that was his name—sat down for breakfast, his servants would come out with baskets, full of gold pieces, and scatter them among the poor.

And when the last gold piece had been scrambled for, King Karan would sit down to his breakfast. (Which I have to tell you consisted of rather more than a crumb of bread or a sip of water.) He was a jolly king, a plump king, an everlastingly hungry king; and of course everybody in his kingdom thought as you do—it couldn't be done. Today, tomorrow, his gold would run out, he wouldn't be able (because of his vow) to eat his breakfast; in short, he would become a gloomy, horribly thin, desperately hungry king, and in no time would die of starvation.

But day after day after day the gold appeared, twenty pounds exactly, and was scattered, and scrambled for, and the king was able to sit down to his breakfast, and every day his servants felt anxious for the same reason—they wondered if he would finish in time to begin his lunch.

Oho, you say, there's a trick in it somewhere. Well, yes. There was a trick in it. On the top of a nearby hill lived an old man who was very holy, a master of magic, and, like the king himself, amazingly hungry. The two of them had come to an agreement.

AGREEMENT BETWEEN HOLY MAN AND KING

Holy man agrees to give king twenty pounds of gold every day.

King agrees to allow himself to be fried and eaten for breakfast every day.

Hold on, you say. Anyone can see that would last one day only. People who get eaten can't expect to come back next day and get eaten again. People who get eaten stay eaten.

But you've forgotten that I said this holy man was a master of magic. He ate the king, he enjoyed eating the king, his stomach deliciously rumbled after he'd eaten the king: and then, having picked the royal bones absolutely clean, he put them together, taking care to get them in the right order, murmured a magic word or two, waved his hands about a bit, and . . . there was King Karan, completely restored: jolly, fat, and enormously ready for his own breakfast.

There *was* a drawback. You'll not have tried it, but you'll easily imagine that there is a nasty side to being popped into an immense frying pan of boiling oil. But King Karan got used to that, and allowed himself to be fried in a very gracious, kingly way: saying a cheerful good morning to the holy man, stepping elegantly into what he tried to think of as an exceptionally hot morning bath: and he even sizzled and frizzled and crackled in a thoroughly royal fashion. Once he was brown all over the holy man sat down to eat him, picked the bones clean, put them together again, murmured his charms, exchanged smiles with the king (who looked as good as ever); and then shook an old coat from the pockets of which gold pieces tumbled onto the floor. The king gathered them up, and back to the palace he went.

Now, in the kingdom next to King Karan's there was a great lake. The lake was home to a flock of wild swans who fed only on pearls. And not just any old pearls: they would eat nothing but *black* pearls. But suddenly there was a shortage of pearls of every kind. So one pair of swans decided to fly to the next kingdom but one and throw themselves on the mercy of the king, who was called Bikru. They landed in the royal garden, to the delight of the royal gardener, who offered them grain to eat, but of course they would have nothing to do with that, or with anything else he offered. So the gardener went to King Bikru and told him about the beautiful swans who would eat nothing.

As it happened, King Bikru spoke the

language of birds: and so he went into the garden and asked the swans why they were turning up their golden beaks when invited to eat.

"Oh," said the swans. "We eat only fresh black pearls."

Any other king might have said that was a very expensive kind of food and that they must try elsewhere. But King Bikru was a kindly king, so he sent for several baskets full of pearls and, every day, fed the swans with his own hand.

But a morning came when one of the pearls was *not* black. It was an ordinary pearly pearl. The two swans decided that King Bikru had run out of black pearls; and they took at once to the air and flew back to the lake, hoping things might have improved there. But they remained grateful to Bikru and, as they flew, they sang a song about him, saying what a good, kind king he was.

Now it happened that they'd chosen a flight path directly over King Karan's palace. "King Bikru is a great man," they were singing. "King Bikru is a kind man. King Bikru is the kindest king there ever was."

King Karan, too, could speak the language of birds: and he was *not* pleased. Here am I, he thought, giving away twenty pounds of gold to the poor every day of my life (and allowing myself to be fried into the bargain), and these birds can only say what a very fine king this other man is.

So King Karan sent for his birdcatchers, and they set out at once to catch the swans, and put them in a cage. They brought them to the king who ordered the birds to be fed with grain, fruit, and every imaginable kind of bird food. But they would have nothing to do with any of it.

"Now, what's this?" said King Karan. "What's wrong with our bird food? You seem to have liked King Bikru's food well enough, judging by that song you were singing. What did he give you that we haven't?"

"That's very simple," said the swans. "He gave us black pearls. We eat only black pearls."

"Very well," said King Karan, "you shall have

black pearls." And he sent for several baskets full of them: but still the swans wouldn't eat.

"And *now* what's wrong?" asked King Karan, becoming rather red in the face.

"King Bikru," said the lady swan, "does not imprison innocent birds in cages. He certainly wouldn't imprison a *lady*. If King Bikru were here, he would let *me* go free, at least."

"What Bikru would do, I can do," said King Karan, and he let the lady swan go; whereupon she flew straight back to King Bikru's garden, and told that kindly king that her husband had been made a prisoner by King Karan.

Now, there were really no limits to King Bikru's kindness. He was heartbroken at the thought of that beautiful swan trapped in a cage and robbed of the companionship of his wife, so he decided to set out at once to rescue the captive. He disguised himself as a serving man, and took the road to King Karan's kingdom. Once there he had no difficulty in persuading the king to take him on as a servant: and soon found himself carrying out the baskets of gold pieces every morning to be scattered among the poor.

"Oho," thought King Bikru to himself (as you said to *yourselves* earlier in this story, if you remember) "there's a trick in it somewhere!" So he kept watch, and early one morning saw King Karan climb up to the holy man's house. He watched him step into the frying pan, and frizzle, sizzle, and crackle, and turn brown (and very crisp), and get himself eaten to the very bones: and get himself put together again, and set off down the hill with his twenty pounds of gold.

"Oho," thought King Bikru again. He knew what he had to do. Next day he got up very early indeed; and taking some pepper, some salt, a variety of spices, an assortment of seeds (including pomegranate), a touch or more of flour, and one or two secret ingredients, he made a gorgeous curry, which he smeared all over himself. There he was a completely curried king! Then he went up the hill, jumped into the frying pan, and began to sizzle, frizzle, and crackle. The

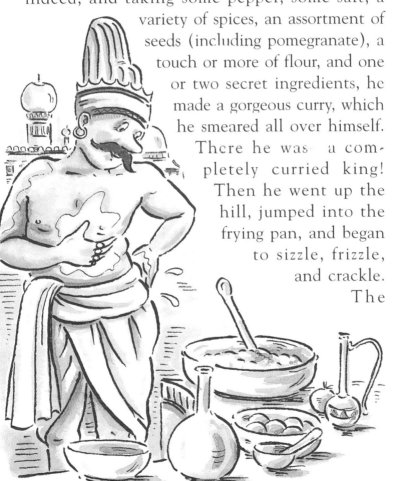

holy man was still asleep, but the appetizing commotion in the frying pan soon woke him up. "I say!" thought the holy man. "King Karan does smell particularly delicious this morning!

I don't know if you've ever eaten quite good food, perfectly enjoyable food for a long time, and then suddenly found yourself eating food so stunning that your stomach would clap and cheer as you ate it, if stomachs could clap and cheer? That's how it was for the holy man, eating this gloriously curried King Bikru! He felt his stomach would have leaped to its feet and thrown its hat in the air, if stomachs had feet and wore hats. His sight was poor, and one king was much like another to him, so he didn't notice he wasn't eating King Karan as usual. He lingered over him, he relished

every mouthful, he made one or two of those rude noises that even holy men can make when they are enjoying what they are eating; and he picked the bones cleaner than he had ever done. In fact, the curry made the bones taste so good that he nearly ate *them*, too! But just in time he told himself that if he did that, there'd be no restoring the king to life and that that would be the last of his marvelous breakfasts. So he put the bones together, and murmured his charms: and to King Bikru (as we know it really was) he said: "That was terrific! *What* a breakfast! If I live to be a thousand!" —actually, he *did* live to be a thousand—"I'll never forget that! How did you manage to taste so nice? Tell me, and I'll give you anything you ask."

So King Bikru told him (pepper, salt, pomegranate seeds, you remember), and promised to curry himself every morning, if only he might have the old coat in return. "You see," he said, "that way I won't have all the bother of carrying the gold down to the palace. If I take the coat, I can shake it when I get down there. You see?"

"I see," said the holy man: and off went King Bikru with the coat.

Oho, you say, we know what happened next. And you're right. Up the hill came King Karan, ready to jump into the frying pan: and very surprised he was to find that the fire was out, the frying pan had been put back in the cupboard, and the holy man, clasping his noisy stomach, was very happy indeed.

"What's all this?" cried King Karan.

"I beg your pardon," said the holy man, who was half-asleep: as anyone might be who'd had curried king for breakfast. "Who are you?"

"What a question!" said the king. "How many years have I been doing this? I'm King Karan, of course, and I've come as usual to be fried. Aren't you hungry?"

"That I am *not*!" said the holy man. "I've already eaten you, thank you very much: *curried!* Marvelous! You were *marvelous*!"

"I've never been curried in my life!" cried King Karan. "Whoever you ate, it wasn't me!"

"Well, I don't much mind who it was," said the holy man, more

and more sleepily. "He . . . was . . . ah! . . . such . . . spiciness!" And he fell deeply asleep.

"Now, you wake up at once!" cried King Karan, shaking him. "Remember our agreement! You've *got* to eat me!"

"Couldn't!" murmured the holy man. "Full up!" He made one of those noises I've mentioned. "Absolutely full up!" And he fell asleep again.

"Look here!" cried King Karan, shaking the holy man quite furiously. "You give me my gold! Remember our agreement! If you don't want to eat me, you must still give me my gold."

"Can't! Very sorry!" murmured the holy man. "Other chap . . . went off with the coat!" And here the holy man fell into a contented sleep so deep that I doubt if anyone could have shaken him awake again.

So back to his palace went King Karan. He was in despair. There was nothing he could do but order his treasurer to send him gold so that, for that morning at least, he could keep his vow and then at last sit down, late and cross, to his breakfast.

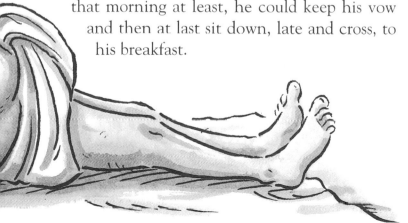

And the next morning, and the morning after that, by scraping together every bit of gold to be found anywhere in the palace, he managed to satisfy the poor, and eat his breakfast. But the morning after *that*, the Royal Treasurer appeared with empty hands, crying: "Your Majesty, alas, alas! Not a bit of gold left! Not a bit!"

So the king went back to bed, with an empty stomach; and the poor, having waited and waited, at last went grumbling away without their gold.

By lunchtime King Karan was already much thinner; by dinnertime he was very thin indeed; by next morning he was but a shadow of himself; and by next lunchtime he was as near to being a skeleton as you can get while you've still got your skin on.

So then King Bikru came to him, carrying the holy man's old coat, and shook it so that gold fell out of the pockets. And King Bikru said, "Here, the money's yours: give it to the poor, and you can have your breakfast." Then he explained who he was and how he had only pretended to be a serving man. "And you can keep the coat, on condition that you set the wild swan free from that cage."

King Karan didn't think twice: he set the swan free, and the happy bird joined his wife in the air, and they set off together to the great lake, singing as they went: "King Bikru is a great man! King

Bikru is a kind man! King Bikru is the kindest king there ever was!" And so on.

And King Karan felt thoroughly ashamed, and said to himself: "They're right!—those swans are right! Bikru is a much better man than I am! I let myself be fried in return for twenty pounds of gold and my breakfast; but he let himself be *curried* so that he might set a bird free from its cage!"

You want to know if he went on letting himself be fried and eating those enormous breakfasts? Well yes, he did: and he lived for a very long time: and they used to say King Karan was probably the

fattest man in his kingdom, though certainly the
second fattest man in the kingdom was the holy
man.

THE HOUSE OF COLORED WINDOWS

Margaret Mahy

Our street had a lot of little houses on either side of it where we children lived happily with our families. There were rows of lawns, like green napkins tucked under the houses' chins, and letterboxes, apple trees, and marigolds. Children played up and down the street, laughing and shouting and sometimes crying, for it's the way of the world that things should be mixed. In the soft autumn evenings, before the winter winds began, the smoke from chimneys rose up in threads of gray and blue, stitching our houses into the autumn air.

But there was one house in our street that was different from all the rest, and that was the wizard's house. For one thing there was a door knocker of iron in the shape of a dog's head that barked at us as we ran by. Of course, the wizard's house had its lawn too, but no apple trees or marigolds, only a silver tree with a golden parrot in it. But that was not the most wonderful thing about the wizard's house.

Once, we saw a tiny dragon sitting on the wizard's compost heap among the apple cores, weeds, and egg shells. He scratched under a green wing with a scarlet claw and breathed out blue flames and gray smoke. We saw the wizard shaking his tablecloth out of the window. Bits of old spells and scraps of magic flew into the air like pink confetti, blue spaghetti, and bits and bobs of rainbow. As they fell, they went off like fireworks and only colored dust reached the ground. The hot sun dissolved the dust as hot tea dissolves sugar. But still those things were not the real wonders of the wizard's house.

The real wonders of the wizard's house were its windows. They were all the colors of the world—red, blue, green, gold, purple and pink, violet and yellow, as well as the reddish-brown of autumn leaves. His house was patched all over with colored windows. And there was not just one pink window or one green one, either, but several of each color, each one different. No one had told us but we all knew that if you looked through the red window you saw a red world. If you looked through the blue window a blue one. The wizard could go into any of these worlds whenever he wished. He was not only the owner of many windows, but the master of many worlds.

My friend, Anthea, longed to go into the wizard's house and spy out through his windows. Other people dreamed of racing bikes and cameras and guitars, but Anthea dreamed of the wizard's windows. She wanted to get into the wizard's house and look through first one window and then another because she was sure that through one of them she must see the world she really wanted to live in. The cotton candy window would show her a world striped like circus time, the golden window would show her a city of towers and domes, dazzling in the sunlight, and every girl who lived there would be a princess with long golden hair. The windows haunted Anthea so much that her eyes ached for magic peepholes into strange and beautiful countries.

One day, as Anthea came home from school, she saw on the footpath outside the wizard's house, sitting by his letterbox, a white cat with one blue eye and one green eye, golden whiskers, and a collar of gold. It winked at her with its blue eye and scrambled through a gap in the hedge, seeming to beckon with its tail. Anthea scrambled after it with a twist and a wriggle and, when she stood up, she was on the other side of the hedge inside the wizard's garden. Her school uniform had been changed into a long, silver dress with little glass bells all over its sleeves, and her school shoes and socks had changed into slippers of scarlet and stockings of green. In front of her stood the wizard, dressed in a white robe with a tiny green dragon crawling around his shoulders. His cat rubbed against his ankles and purred.

"So, you are the girl who dreams of looking through my windows," said the wizard. "Your wishes are like storms, my dear—too strong, too strong. At night I am beginning to dream your dreams instead of my own and that won't do, for wizards need their own dreams to prevent them becoming lost in their magic. Dreams are to wizards what harbor lights are to a sailor. I'll let you look through my windows, and choose the world you like best of all, so long as you remember that when you walk out of my door you'll walk out into the world you have chosen, and there'll be no coming back a second time. Be sure you choose well."

Anthea followed the wizard up the path between borders of prize-winning geraniums and in at his door.

"This is a lovely dress," she said to the wizard. "I feel halfway to being a princess already. It's much, much nicer than my school uniform."

"But it *is* a school uniform—the uniform of *my* school," the wizard replied in surprise. "I'm glad you like it. Now, here is the red window. Look well, my dear."

Anthea looked through the red window. She was looking deep into a forest on the sun. Trees blazed up from a wide plain and over a seething hillside. Their leaves were flames, and

scarlet smoke rose up from the forest, filling the sky. Out from under the trees galloped a herd of fiery horses, tossing burning manes and tails and striking sparks from the ground with their smoldering hooves.

"Well?" asked the wizard.

"It's beautiful," breathed Anthea, "but it's much too hot."

The next window was a silver one. A princess, with a young face and long white hair, rode through a valley of snow in a silver sleigh drawn by six great white bears wearing collars of frost and diamonds. All around her, mountains rose like needles of silver ice into a blue, clear sky.

"Your silver window is beautiful," Anthea sighed, "but, oh—how cold, how cold! I couldn't live there."

Through a cotton candy-pink window, sure

enough, she looked into a world of circuses. A pink circus tent opened like a spring tree in blossom. Clowns turned cartwheels around it, and a girl in a pink dress and pink slippers rode on a dappled horse, jumping through a hoop hung with pink ribbons.

"That's funny!" Anthea said in a puzzled voice. "It's happy and funny and very, very pretty, but I wouldn't want to live with a circus every day. I don't know why not, but I just wouldn't."

That's how it was with all the windows. The blue one looked under the sea, and the green one into a world of treetops. There was a world of deserts and a world of diamonds, a world of caves and glowworms, and a world of sky with floating cloud-castles, but Anthea did not want to live in any of them. She began to run from one window to another, the glass bells on her sleeves jingling and tinkling, her feet in the scarlet slippers sliding under her.

"Where is a window for me?" cried Anthea. She peered through windows into lavender worlds full of mist, worlds where grass grew up to the sky and spiders spun bridges with rainbow-colored silk, into worlds where nothing grew and where great stones lay like a city of abandoned castles reaching from one horizon to another.

At last there were no windows left. The wizard's house had many, many windows, but Anthea had looked through them all and there was no world in which she wanted to live. She didn't want a hot one or a cold one, a wet one or a dry one. She didn't want a world of trees or a world of stones. The wizard shrugged his shoulders.

"You're hard to please," he said.

"But I wanted the very best one. I know I'd know the best one if only you'd let me see it. Isn't there one window left? One little window?"

"Funnily enough there is one window, but I didn't think you'd be interested," the wizard said.

"You see . . ."

"Please show it to me," begged Anthea.

"I ought to explain . . ." began the wizard.

"Please!" cried Anthea.

The wizard pointed at a little blue-and-white checked curtain. "Behind there," he said.

Anthea ran to pull it aside and found herself looking through a window as clear as a drop of rainwater. She saw a little street with little houses on either side of it. Smoke went up, up, up, stitching the street into the fall sky, and up and down the footpath children ran, shouting and laughing, though some were also crying. There was a woman very like Anthea's own mother, looking for someone very like Anthea, because dinner was ready and there were sausages and mashed potatoes waiting to be eaten.

"That's the one!" cried Anthea, delighted.

"Why did you keep it until last? I've wasted a lot of time on other windows when this one was the best all the time."

Without waiting another moment, she ran out the wizard's door; squeezed through the hedge and found herself in the street wearing her own school uniform again.

"Well, that's funny!" said the wizard to his cat. "Did you see that? She went back to the world she came out of in the first place. That's her mother taking her home for dinner. I must say they do look very happy."

Ten minutes later the white cat with the gold collar brought him a tray with his dinner on it. The wizard looked pleased.

"Oh boy!" he said, because he was having sausages and mashed potatoes, too.

And that night the wizard dreamed his own dreams once more, while Anthea dreamed of a racing bike. And in the darkness, the wizard's house of many windows twinkled like a good spell amid the street lights that marched like bright soldiers down our street.

TITLES IN THE TREASURY SERIES